MOTORCYCLE MANIAC

"The pits!" Joe suddenly slammed his hand on the van's dashboard.

"You mean the old quarry outside of town, where Biker used to practice motocross?" Frank asked. "Let's check it out."

Frank and Joe began to search the quarry, but they didn't see even a trace that Biker Conway had been there.

Then the sudden roar of an engine cut the air. Frank saw a big black cycle ridden by a black-clad figure drive straight toward Joe. There was no time for thinking—only for acting. Frank leapt for Joe.

Joe fell to the ground, hard, then jumped to his feet as the motorcycle roared past him. "That guy nearly ran us down, Frank," he said angrily.

There was no answer.

Frank lay facedown in the dirt, motionless, a thin line of blood trickling down the side of his head.

Books in The Hardy Boys™ Casefiles Series

THE HARDY BOYS CASEFILES NO. 27

NOWHERE TO RUN

FRANKLIN W. DIXON

AN ARCHWAY PAPERBACK
Published by SIMON & SCHUSTER
New York   London   Toronto   Sydney   Tokyo

An Archway paperback
first published in Great Britain
by Simon & Schuster Ltd in 1992
A Paramount Communications Company

Simon & Schuster Ltd
West Garden Place
Kendal Street
London W2 2AQ

Simon & Schuster of Australia Pty Ltd
Sydney

A CIP catalogue record for this book is
available from the British Library

ISBN 0-671-71617-4

Printed and bound in Great Britain by
HarperCollins Manufacturing.

NOWHERE TO RUN

Chapter

1

"SURE YOU CAN have this back—if you're man enough to take it from me." Swinging from the saddle of his 1000 cc Harley-Davidson motorcycle, the stranger held out the bright green Frisbee to Joe Hardy. The biker was dressed in black from helmet to boots, his face masked by a black reflective visor.

"What's your problem? Did the Darth Vader School for Rejects let out early today?" Joe Hardy's blue eyes hardened as he walked over to face off against the black-clad stranger.

An eerie laugh echoed from beneath the Darth Vader helmet and visor, as the biker teased Joe. He tossed the Frisbee into the air and caught it several times.

"Little Joe Hardy thinks he's all grown up now," the guy scoffed.

Joe's face turned an angry red. Six feet tall and well muscled, Joe Hardy was anything but little.

"Just toss him the Frisbee and move on," Frank Hardy spoke up, standing beside his brother. He was an inch taller but leaner than Joe.

"You think the two of you can take this from me?" The stranger swung his leg over the Harley, pushed down the kickstand, and stepped away from the bike to confront Frank and Joe.

The guy stood as tall as Joe and appeared every bit as strong. Something about his swagger seemed familiar to Joe, who took a careful look at the cycle. The biker took advantage of Joe's shift of attention to fire the Frisbee at him.

Joe batted the plastic disk aside and started to jump for the stranger. He was stunned when Frank stiff-armed him to a halt.

"Let's make this a little more even," Frank suggested. "Take off your helmet."

The stranger laughed again and unsnapped his chin strap. Slowly he lifted the helmet from his head. . . .

Minutes earlier, Frank, Joe, and Frank's girl-friend, Callie Shaw, had been enjoying a lazy afternoon at Bayport Park, tossing the Frisbee around. It was the first real rest for Frank and Joe since getting back from Alaska after their last case, *Trouble in the Pipeline*. They'd gone up looking for a missing person and found themselves tangling with terrorists. Now they were home, and things were getting back to normal.

"I hope Mom and Aunt Gertrude get home from vacation soon," Joe had said as he tossed the Frisbee to Frank. "I'm getting a little tired of Dad's frozen fish sticks every night."

"Dad" was the famous private detective Fenton Hardy. Although his sons admired him as a top investigator, they were not impressed with his talent as a cook.

"I know what you mean." Frank jumped to catch Joe's toss. "I looked in the mirror this morning and thought I saw gills." He whipped the Frisbee around his back and fired it at Callie.

"Don't worry." Callie grinned as she caught Frank's pass with the tip of her finger and let it spin for a few seconds. "*I'll* fix you dinner tonight. How does Caesar salad and lasagna sound?"

"Oh, Callie," Joe teased. "I knew you were good for something."

That got him a dirty look from Callie—as well as a rocketing Frisbee aimed straight at his throat.

"Hey!" Joe backpedaled and cushioned the blow of the Frisbee against his chest. He leapt into the air, whirled around, and tossed the Frisbee between his legs. It sailed wildly over Callie's head and landed on the park's motorcycle trail.

"Nice throw, Joe," Callie said, fuming.

Joe brushed back his blond hair. "Sorry, Callie." He didn't sound too sorry, though.

Callie jogged over to pick up the Frisbee, but she never reached it. The black-clad biker had screamed to a stop and snatched up the plastic disk. He refused to give it to Callie. Sensing trouble, Frank and Joe had run to Callie's aid.

Now Joe stood poised, ready to jump this hood the moment he made his move. The stranger pulled the helmet from his head.

Frank gasped.

But Joe yelled in joyful surprise. "Biker, you maniac!" He did jump on the guy now, but only to slap him on the back. "What are you doing back in Bayport?"

"Biker?" asked a confused Callie.

"Bob Conway, senorita bonita," the cyclist said. " 'Biker' to my friends." He gave her a disarming smile. Callie looked confused.

"Biker's an old friend of Joe's," Frank said. "He graduated from Bayport High three years ago."

"This guy was my hero when I was a kid," Joe explained. "He's the one who taught me about hot-rodding engines and racing motorcycles." His grin stretched from ear to ear. "Biker was a champion motocross racer on the junior circuit when I was a freshman.''

"It was the only way I could get you out of my hair.'' Biker laughed and said to Callie, "He'd hang around the garage where I worked and bug me until I showed him a few tricks. He was a good student.''

"My dad said Joe got his temper from you, too,'' Frank added with a laugh.

"Yeah, well, you've got a great dad, but I'll never understand why he was always angry at me,'' Biker said.

"Probably because of stunts like this,'' Callie said as she picked up the Frisbee.

"Oh, that,'' Biker said. He looked a little embarrassed. "I couldn't help myself. Besides, I know the Hardys are always up for a little adventure. And you have to admit, Joe looked pretty silly standing there ready to fight over a Frisbee.''

Callie stared at him, squinting as she tried to dredge something out of her memory. "Wait a second,'' she said. "Didn't you go to jail or something?''

"He was innocent.'' Joe's voice rose. "And we helped prove it.''

"Be cool, Joe,'' Biker said.

"It was something about stealing motorcycle parts,'' Callie went on.

Joe's face reddened with anger. "I told you—''

"Hey, wait a minute—you're Callie Shaw.''

Biker smiled, his soft brown eyes staring into Callie's. "I used to tell Joe that you were the cutest freshman at Bayport High."

Callie blushed.

"Three years ago, right before graduating, I was arrested for buying stolen cycle parts," Biker explained. "The dirt-cheap prices should have warned me, but I was a little thickheaded back then. About a week before I went on trial, Frank and Joe caught the real thieves and cleared me. I graduated from BHS and went off to make my fortune."

"You're going to stick around for a few days, aren't you?" Joe asked.

"Time is about all I have left," Biker replied with a slight smile.

Frank sensed Biker was holding something back.

"You can stay with us," Joe added. He knew Biker's folks had moved out of Bayport.

Biker glanced around. "You're sure you want an escaped convict sleeping in your house?"

"*What?*" Joe stared—so did Frank and Callie.

"Is this another dumb prank?" Callie demanded.

" 'Fraid not." Biker threw a leg back over his bike and sank down on the saddle.

"If you're telling the truth," Frank said, "we shouldn't even be talking with you."

"What are you saying?" Joe turned on his brother.

Biker nodded. "He's saying that aiding an escaped felon could get you into trouble—serious trouble."

"Never mind that." Joe brushed the idea aside. "How can we help?"

Frank looked unhappily at his brother, not liking Joe's eagerness. "First tell us what happened," he said.

"After I left Bayport," Biker began, "I cycled up and down the East Coast. Finally I settled in New York City. I got a job as a mechanic at a small watch company out in Queens called Dal-Time. One day a sales representative got sick and I took his place."

He shrugged. "The next thing I knew, I was selling designer watches. Last year DalTime's Watch Ya Wearing? was the top sports watch in the country—and I was the top salesperson."

"Sounds as if you made your fortune," Frank said.

"Yeah, but the fame that came with it wasn't exactly what I had in mind." Biker sighed. "Three months ago I returned from a cross-country bike trip, right into the arms of a welcoming committee. Two of New York's finest." Callie didn't understand and looked confused. "Two cops," Biker explained. "I was arrested, tried, and convicted of hijacking a shipment of DalTime watches valued at half a million bucks.''

Joe whistled.

"Based on what evidence?" Frank asked.

"Oh, little things." Biker was trying hard to look calm, but there was fire in his eyes. "They found a sudden increase of twenty-five thousand dollars in my bank account and several boxes of Watch Ya Wearing? watches in my garage. The serial numbers just happened to match the ones on the invoice for the stolen watches."

"That's all?" Frank asked.

"Yes, if you don't count the eyewitness."

"Eyewitness?" Callie couldn't believe what she was hearing.

"Yeah. The truck driver managed to convince everybody that I was the hijacker." Biker paused. "Even though the hijacker was wearing a mask."

"This begins to sound like a frame to me," Joe said.

"How did you escape?" Frank asked.

"I was on the way to the state prison at Attica, and—remember that little lock-picking trick you taught me, Frank?"

Joe grinned, remembering how Frank had challenged Biker to get out of a pair of handcuffs.

"The cops' cuffs were actually easier to pick than the ones you had me practice on." Biker broke up at the expression on Frank's face.

"So now you're here." Callie obviously didn't like the idea.

"I sneaked back into the company and got a charge card to buy a bike and riding gear. I also got some cash. I plan to pay them back. At first I thought of heading to Canada; then I thought of Frank and Joe."

"What can they do for you?" Callie demanded.

"Look, I'm innocent—and I need help to prove it."

"Count on us," Joe said, ignoring the troubled look on Frank's face. "The first thing we have to do is crack the driver's story."

Frank glanced from Joe to Biker. "I don't know," he said.

Joe turned to Frank. "You believe him, don't you?

"That's not what's bothering me." Frank looked Biker in the eye. "If we take you in, we're harboring an escaped felon."

Biker shrugged again and got back on his Harley. "Gotcha. I owe you guys too much to get you into trouble with the law." He kicked his hog to life.

"Wait a minute!" Joe yelled. "We can talk this over."

"We could use Dad's advice on this," Frank said and paused. "Well, we could talk, I guess— on one condition."

"Name it," Biker said.

"Tell our dad your story, then turn yourself in. You're not doing yourself any good by running." Frank braced himself for a fight—not with Biker but with Joe. Once Joe got an idea in his head, he could be deadly stubborn.

"Wait a minute—" Joe began.

Biker cut in, "Your father's fair. If he'll listen to me, I can't go wrong—not with three Hardys helping me."

After dropping Callie off at her house, Frank and Joe drove home in their van, followed by Biker on his Harley.

"What's that old wreck doing across the street?" Frank asked as he pulled into the Hardy driveway.

"Huh?" Joe had been deep in thought.

"I've never seen that beat-up old Chevy around here before," Frank said.

"I'm more interested in what we're going to tell Dad," Joe said. "He never really liked Biker."

Biker pulled up beside the van and slipped off his cycle.

They were almost to the front door when it burst open and a short, plump man stepped out on the porch. Frank and Joe had never seen him before.

"Freeze, turkeys," the man snarled, his voice like gravel on concrete.

Frank nearly broke up. The guy sounded like a bad imitation of a TV detective.

One thing was for real, though—the hair-trigger 9 mm automatic pistol the man had aimed right at Biker's head.

Chapter

2

"No!" BIKER YELLED, shoving Frank and Joe aside and dashing back to his bike.

The short, heavy man shouldered past the Hardys. Joe watched in horror as the man braced himself in a firing position, taking aim as Biker swung onto the Harley.

Hurling himself at the stranger, Joe tackled him just as the gun went off. The shot buried itself in the lawn. Biker's cycle screamed with power, and he tore off down the street.

Joe jumped to his feet only to find himself looking down the barrel of the pistol.

"All right, punk," the short man wheezed. "You want it the hard way?"

"Hey!" Frank shouted.

12

The man looked like a joke, but he moved like a pro. He pivoted, covering both Frank and Joe. "Down on the ground," he ordered. "Facedown. *Move!*"

"Sims! Put that gun down!" shouted Fenton Hardy, running through the doorway. "These are my sons."

"Your sons?" Sims asked in confusion, still flicking his gun between Frank and Joe.

"Yes, and getting shot might be bad for their health."

Sims lowered his gun, sliding the deadly automatic into its shoulder holster.

"Your sons walked up with Biker Conway. They helped him escape," Sims said. "You didn't tell me they were so buddy-buddy with crooks."

Joe went for Sims, but Frank grabbed his arm and pulled him back. "Who is this guy?" he asked.

"First let's get inside," Fenton said.

Once in the living room, the elder Hardy began the introductions and explanations. "This is Mort Sims. Sims, these are my sons, Frank and Joe."

Neither the Hardys nor Sims offered to shake hands. The tension in the air was thick.

"Sims is a private investigator from New York City," Fenton went on. "He's looking for Bob Conway."

"I *had* him until Joe jumped me. I would have stopped him, too."

"Stopped him?" Joe shot back. "You were going to blow him away!"

"Listen, sonny, I've been hired to nail him. Nobody cares *how* I bring him in."

Frank saw a muscle just above Joe's jaw flex and took a step to place himself between Sims and his younger brother. He didn't like Sims's attitude, but he wanted more information from the private detective.

"Who hired you?" Frank asked with a quick glance at Joe. Joe recognized his brother's silent signal to cool it and relaxed.

"Scott Dalton, founder and president of Dal-Time, the watch company Conway stole from."

"Why? Biker's innocent." Joe couldn't keep the words in.

"Yeah? Who made you judge and jury? Mr. Dalton had complete faith in Conway, even put up three hundred grand in bail money so Conway could be free during his trial. The old man was willing to help with Conway's appeal, too, until Conway escaped. Now the bail money's been forfeited, *and* Conway's charged on the company card. Mr. Dalton wants either Conway or his money back."

Joe stared at Sims as if he were some kind of very ugly bug. "You're nothing but a bounty hunter," he said.

14

Sims clamped his jaw. Joe had hit a nerve.

"What are you doing here?" Frank asked, trying to catch Sims off balance.

Sims laughed. "It's no secret that Conway's from Bayport. I figured I'd check the place out—and ask an old friend from the New York force to help look for this escaped con." Sims glanced at Fenton Hardy.

"Wh-what?" Joe stared at his father.

"Sims doesn't know Bayport," Fenton explained. "I'm a consultant on this case."

"But you can't—" Joe began.

"Can't what? Can't uphold the law?" Sims threw himself into a chair, the springs groaning under his bulk. "Can't be a bounty hunter?"

Frank saw that Joe was ready to jump on Sims again, and gave his brother a jab in the ribs. Joe glared back.

"What were you two doing with Conway?" Fenton asked.

Frank looked at Joe, then answered for both of them.

"We met him in the park about an hour ago," Frank said. "He explained about the robbery and wanted us to clear him. We were bringing him here, hoping you could help."

"He was thinking of turning himself in before Wyatt Earp here began waving his gun around," Joe added. His cold blue eyes bored into Sims.

"You were doing the right thing," Fenton said.

15

"But if you see Biker again, restrain him and call me. This is Sims's case, and he's within the law. In spite of your feelings, Joe, Biker is a convicted felon."

"Yeah. Let older, wiser heads handle this job," Sims added with a sarcastic smile.

Joe turned to Fenton. "You never did like Biker."

"What I didn't like," Fenton replied, an edge in his voice, "was his hot temper—and the way his wildness rubbed off on you."

"You won't even think about his side of this," Joe said, frustrated. "Look at the case against him. The watches were planted in Biker's garage, and anybody can deposit money into a bank account. It's obvious that the eyewitness was lying."

Sims jumped up to stand toe-to-toe with Joe.

"Just like that!" he shouted with a snap of his fingers. "You solved the case. You've decided that a judge and jury didn't do their jobs right— no, you know better." Sims stabbed a plump finger at Joe's chest. "Every punk in Queens knows you don't run out on the law. If you do, you answer to Mort Sims. My job is to bring Conway back—dead or alive!"

Joe exploded. He pushed Sims backward. Caught off guard, Sims fell over the chair. But on the way down he lashed out with a karate kick, knocking Joe's legs out from under him.

Frank and Fenton stepped between the two. "Break it up," Fenton snapped. Frank pushed Joe out the front door.

Before following Joe, Frank faced his father. "He'll cool down in a little while. In the meantime we'll be at Mr. Pizza."

"You understand what I said about dealing with Conway," Fenton said.

Frank paused in the doorway. "We understand," he said. "But we don't have to like it."

The boys drove in absolute silence. Both brothers were thinking. Joe didn't like the idea of his father working with a bounty hunter to trap one of his best friends. He knew he *had* to prove Biker's innocence before trigger-happy Sims got him in his sights again.

Frank's eyes flicked between the road ahead and Joe. His brother often blew up, and he usually could shrug it off quickly. But that wasn't happening. Now Joe seemed filled with cold fury.

A chilling thought flashed through Frank's mind. If it came down to a choice, would Joe stand by his friend and idol, Biker Conway, or his father, who had teamed up with a bounty hunter? Frank became determined that such a decision shouldn't have to be made.

"The pits!" Joe suddenly slammed his hand on the dashboard.

"I know," Frank replied. "But we'll solve this one—"

"No," Joe interrupted. "Remember the pits? Where Biker used to practice?"

"You mean the old quarry outside of town?"

"Yeah. He could be camping there."

Frank shook his head. "Too obvious."

"Only if you know that Biker used to practice there, and Sims doesn't know Bayport, remember?" Joe looked at his brother. "It's worth a try."

"Okay, we'll check it out." Frank turned the van toward the pits.

Joe smiled. Just as he'd done three years earlier, he intended to clear Biker of a crime. He would put Sims in his place and prove to his father that Biker wasn't a thief.

The pits consisted of five square miles of large and small holes left after a mining company had dug out all the profitable sandstone. The area of dirt and stones looked more like a moonscape or an air force bombing range than a part of Bayport. But it made a great motocross practice course.

Frank and Joe parked the van, then split up and began to search from opposite ends of the quarry.

Joe's high hopes of finding Biker at the pits soon vanished. He didn't see even a trace of evidence that Conway had been there. Frustrated, Joe kicked up a cloud of dust.

"Hey!" Frank yelled as he jogged toward Joe. "I saw your smoke signals."

"Find anything?" Joe asked, an expectant look on his face.

"Nothing. You?"

Joe shook his head.

"It's getting dark," Frank said with a glance at the sky. "I called Callie on the mobile phone, and she's going to meet us at Mr. Pizza in half an hour. Let's eat something and brainstorm."

"Yeah," Joe grunted and headed for the van.

Frank shook his head. After girl-collecting, eating good food was Joe's favorite pastime. When even an invitation to a hot pizza supreme couldn't cheer Joe up, he was in a bad way.

The sudden roar of an engine cut the air. Frank saw a big black cycle swerve out from behind a gravel mound and drive toward Joe. Lost in thought, Joe didn't notice the cycle or its black-clad rider.

The cyclist had noticed Joe, though. He was aiming straight for him, hefting something in his hand.

Frank stared for one quick second, wondering what was behind that reflective helmet. Then there was no time for thinking—only for acting. He leapt for Joe.

Joe felt someone shove him from behind, so hard that he was lifted into the air before he fell—hard—to the ground. He jumped to his feet as a motorcycle roared past him and out of the quarry.

"That guy nearly ran us down," he said angrily. "You get his license number, Frank?"

When he got no answer, Joe spun around.

Frank lay facedown in the dirt, motionless, a thin line of blood trickling down the side of his head.

Chapter

3

JOE'S EYES WIDENED. "Frank!" he yelled, dropping to one knee.

He gingerly brushed away the dust from his brother's head. The bleeding had almost stopped, but the area around the gash was starting to swell. What could have caused this? Joe wondered.

Then he saw a small crowbar lying on the ground. "Another inch and it would have been over," he muttered.

He pressed a handkerchief against Frank's temple.

"Ouch!" Frank's eyes fluttered open.

"You'll have a good lump there." Joe gave his brother a quick smile.

But Frank didn't smile back. "Did you see who was driving that bike?"

"Couldn't tell. First I wasn't paying any attention. Then the only thing I saw was dust." Joe picked up the crowbar and examined it. "This is a standard motorcycle tool."

"Think it might have been Biker?" Frank forced the question out.

Joe's eyes flashed. "No way. Why would he do that?"

"I saw our attacker—he had the same type of motorcycle, same clothes. Who else do we know who dresses like that?"

Joe frowned. "I didn't see anything. But I did hear the engine. It sounded terrible."

"I was too busy saving you to listen. What does the sound of the engine mean?"

Joe walked over to the tire tracks and followed them around the gravel mound. "Over here!" he yelled at Frank.

Joe squatted down beside a black stain that stood out in the dead gray dirt of the quarry. He pinched some of the black stuff and rubbed it between his fingers.

"Oil," he announced. "And it's hot, as if it had just leaked out of a running engine." He glanced around, then smiled. "Notice anything about the tire tracks?"

"The tires are worn down, as if they'd been on a long trip." Frank was growing impatient.

"Worn down?" Joe said. "They're bald. And the footprints next to them prove that the driver was wearing regular street shoes."

"What's the point?"

"You know Biker. He wouldn't ride his cycle with an oil leak like this, or let his tires wear down. And he wouldn't wear street shoes even for casual riding. He may not be serious about a lot of things, but cycling is his religion."

"That was three years ago." Frank folded his arms across his chest.

"Don't give me that big-brother routine," Joe spat out angrily. "You did that the last time I wanted to help Biker, and you looked pretty foolish then, too.

Frank looked at the oil spot and the tire tracks and footprints. Then he looked at his brother.

"Okay," he said with a sigh. "I'll go along with you for now. I just want to be sure that we aren't on the wrong side of the law this time. But if it wasn't Biker, who was it?"

"Maybe the same person who framed Biker. Someone who wants to stop us from proving he's innocent."

"Or someone who wants to nail Biker before we can help him," Frank countered.

"What?"

"No one knew we were coming out here. We came looking for Biker. I'd guess whoever attacked us must have been waiting for Biker, too.

"We've got to find Biker and warn him." Joe raced for the van.

"First, let's get Callie at Mr. Pizza," Frank said as he hopped in the passenger door.

"She'll just get in the way," Joe protested.

"We can find Biker faster with three of us looking," Frank replied sternly. Even after all Callie had done to help the Hardys, Joe was still reluctant to involve her. Maybe it was because she was Frank's girlfriend. Or maybe it was simply because she was a girl.

The cool air of the Bayport Mall was a welcome relief to Frank's throbbing head. He didn't like Joe's automatic defense of Biker. If he began to get desperate, Joe might just do something stupid. Best to find Biker, get him to a safe place, and then concentrate on finding their attacker.

They walked into Mr. Pizza, the aroma of spices, cheese, and pepperoni reminding them that they hadn't eaten. Callie was waiting at their favorite booth, impatiently tapping her straw on an empty soda glass.

"It's about time you two—" Callie began. Then she noticed the lump on Frank's temple. "What happened?" she gasped.

Frank quickly explained about meeting Mort Sims and their encounter in the pits with the mysterious rider.

"I think your father's right," Callie said. "It

24

looks as if Biker causes trouble wherever he goes."

"His main trouble is getting blamed for stuff by people who don't know him," Joe shot back.

"Settle down, Joe," Frank said with a frown. "No need to start jumping down our throats."

"Everyone's treating Biker like a hardened criminal," Joe said. "How can he expect us to help him if Callie and Dad are trying to put him back in jail?"

"I didn't say I wanted him back in jail," Callie said. "I only—"

"Excuse me," interrupted a tall, dark-haired young man wearing a leather cycle jacket. "The manager said you two are Frank and Joe Hardy."

The guy's jacket didn't really go with his pretty-boy good looks. He actually had a dimple in his chin, and his hair was carefully styled.

Joe was ready to tell the guy to beat it when he noticed a pretty auburn-haired girl standing next to him. Her blue jumpsuit showed off a great figure, and her green eyes were fixed on Joe—a nice feeling, since she had to be twenty-one or twenty-two.

"Can we help you?" Frank asked cordially, relieved that the verbal battle between Joe and Callie had reached a temporary cease-fire.

"My name is Brandon Dalton. This is Sue Murphy," he said with a nod toward the auburn-haired girl.

25

"Hi." Sue gave them a shy smile.

"Dalton," said Frank thoughtfully. "Any relation to Scott Dalton?"

"My father," Brandon replied. "You must be Frank." He stuck his hand out toward the older Hardy. "And you must be Joe. I'm told you're just about the best detectives around."

Brandon's pale blue eyes rested on Callie. "And who's your friend?" he asked with a big smile.

"This is Callie Shaw," Frank said, aware of Brandon's admiring stare at Callie.

"Who told you we were detectives?" Joe asked as Brandon and Sue squeezed into the booth.

"A close friend of both of ours," Brandon said. "Biker Conway. He means a lot to us at the watch company, and we want to find him before Sims does."

"Yeah. I'm—we're afraid that if Sims finds Biker first—well . . ." Sue's voice broke off.

"Sims has a rotten reputation," Brandon said flatly. "We want to make sure Biker doesn't get hurt."

"How did you know we were here?" Frank asked.

"We stopped off at your house and spoke with your father," Brandon replied. "Sims told my dad yesterday that he suspected Biker might hide out in Bayport. We—that is, Sue and I—decided to follow him and make sure Sims brings Biker

26

back in one piece." Brandon leaned back, unzipping his riding jacket. "You see, I'm his best friend, and Sue is his fiancée."

Joe felt a pang of disappointment. Then he silently congratulated Biker on having great taste in women.

"I'm the vice-president in charge of sales," Brandon said, folding his arms over his chest. "Sue works in the records and accounts section. I persuaded my dad to put up the bail money. No one really believed that Biker stole that shipment of watches, but when he escaped and used the company's charge account for running money, my dad blew his top. He hired this Sims character to track Biker down."

Brandon shook his head. "In Queens, they call Sims 'Old Dead-or-Alive.' He's a real hard-nosed character."

"We want to try to find Biker, talk him into coming back to appeal his case," Sue added softly, leaning forward.

"That's what we had in mind," Joe said. He liked the smile Sue gave him. "I don't think Frank and I will have too much trouble discrediting the evidence."

"We're not sure what we're going to do yet," Frank said, more to Joe than to anyone else.

"I don't know—the evidence seemed pretty conclusive," Brandon said. "The defense attorney did say that the money in the bank account and the watches in Biker's garage could have been planted. But after Nick Frost testified, everyone seemed convinced that Biker was guilty."

"Nick Frost?" Frank murmured to himself as if he had heard the name before somewhere.

"He was the driver of the truck that was hijacked—the eyewitness," Brandon said.

"He lied," Joe growled.

"To prove that, we'll have to find Frost," Sue said.

"He's missing?" Callie asked.

"About the same time that Biker escaped, Frost disappeared also," Brandon said. He suddenly rose. "If you'll excuse me, I have to call the company and check in with my dad."

"There's a pay phone by the counter," Callie told him.

"Thanks, babe." Brandon winked, and Callie blushed a deep red.

"Have you known Biker long?" Joe asked Sue.

"Almost three years." Sue stared at the table, twisting a paper napkin in her hands. "Practically from the day he began working at DalTime. At first I thought he was just a macho jerk."

"What made you change your mind?" Callie asked. Joe glared at her, but she just wrinkled her nose at him.

"Underneath all that leather and motorcycle oil is a gentle, caring man."

"When do you plan on being married?" Callie went on.

"Callie . . ." Joe said sternly.

Sue fought back a sob. "Last week." She wiped her eyes with the napkin and turned to Joe, a fragile smile on her face. "Biker told me a lot about you."

"Really?"

"Yes. When he was teaching me about bike riding, he'd tell stories about this gawky kid who used to bug him about engines."

Joe felt his face turn hot from embarrassment.

"I think he made most of it up," Sue said.

"Was there any evidence that Biker was innocent?" Frank wanted to get back on track.

"I was called as a defense witness." Sue turned to Frank, her voice low. "Biker had been—" Sue finished her sentence in a scream.

Frank, Joe, and Callie turned to look where Sue was staring.

Biker Conway had Brandon Dalton pinned to the floor, his fist drawn back to let loose with a crushing blow.

Chapter

4

TONY PRITO, the manager of Mr. Pizza, was the first to reach Biker and Brandon. He grabbed for Biker first, but Biker shrugged him off, thrusting Tony against the counter.

"Tony—" Frank began as he came up.

Tony was a friend of the Hardys, but right then his temper was up. "You know this clown? Well, tell him I'm calling security." Tony jumped over the counter and picked up his phone.

"Biker, stop!" Joe yelled.

"Back off, Joe," Biker growled. "This is between me and Dalton."

Joe was stunned by the fury in Biker's voice.

Dalton's handsome face was white with fear.

30

He looked at Frank with pleading eyes. "Get this maniac off me!"

"This isn't doing you any good," Frank said. The growing crowd of gawkers worried him.

"I'm tired of everyone telling me what's good for me." Biker's fist was still cocked, but he hadn't punched yet.

"The security guards are on their way, pal," Tony shouted from behind the counter.

"Let's get out of here, Biker," Joe said quickly. Biker wouldn't budge.

"Biker, please." Sue's voice was the only calm element in the rising storm.

Biker looked up, embarrassed. He lowered his fist and stood. Frank pulled Brandon up.

"Here come the guards," someone yelled.

Joe grabbed Biker's jacket sleeve and jerked him out the back exit of Mr. Pizza.

"Joe!" Frank shouted. He let go of Brandon and bolted after his brother. Joe's impulsiveness would lead him straight to jail.

Frank plunged down a dark flight of stairs to the loading dock. Voices led him toward the indoor parking garage of the mall. As he sprinted past a support pillar, an arm reached out and grabbed him around the throat.

"Joe! Hold it! It's Frank," yelled Biker.

Joe let go of his brother. "Sorry. I thought you were one of the security men."

"And what if I was?" Frank shouted. "Would you have punched me out?"

"I might have," Joe shouted back.

"What's wrong with you?"

"I'm trying to help Biker."

"How? By helping him escape? Remember what Dad said. We're to hold on to him and call Sims."

"You think turning Biker over to that bounty hunter is a good idea?" Joe's face turned a blazing red. "You heard what Dalton said about that guy."

"That's not our decision."

"Biker was framed!"

"I agree with you, Joe. But we've got to do this the right way or we could all end up in jail. In the eyes of the law, Biker's still an escaped felon. You're helping him escape."

"And you're turning your back on a friend, handing him over to a bloodthirsty bounty hunter."

Frank shoved Joe back against a Dumpster. Brother or not, Joe wasn't going to accuse him of being a coward or betraying a friend. Joe charged Frank.

Biker stepped in, holding the brothers away from each other. "Knock it off, you two. I don't need this kind of help."

Frank and Joe stared at each other until they heard running footsteps.

Callie came dashing up. Breathless, she gasped, "The security guys just entered Mr. Pizza. They'll be heading down here in a second."

Without hesitation, Joe and Biker raced for the van in the parking lot.

"You stay with Sue and Brandon," Frank said to Callie. "See if you can find out more about them and Biker." He backed toward the van. "I'll call you as soon as I can straighten out this crazy mess."

By the time Frank reached the van, Joe had slipped on Biker's jacket and gloves, and had the key's to Biker's cycle clutched in his hand.

"What do you think you're doing?" Frank asked.

"No time," Joe said, slipping on the black helmet and visor.

Two security men were coming down the stairs. One pointed at the group, and both men ran for them.

"You take Biker for a ride," Joe ordered, his voice reverberating in the echo chamber of the helmet. "I'll call you on the mobile phone once I get rid of the guards." He dashed to Biker's Harley before Frank could protest.

Frank made a move toward Joe, but decided against it as the guards drew closer. He hopped into the van and fired it up. He put the van in drive but kept his foot on the brake.

"What are we waiting for?" Biker asked.

"We're not going to leave Joe here if he can't get away," Frank replied.

Joe jumped on the Harley and jammed the key into the ignition. He punched the start button and the engine rumbled to life. The guards changed direction, turning from the van to the bike. Joe kicked up the stand. The guards were only twenty yards away. He squeezed in the hand clutch, pushed the foot lever to first, and twisted the throttle full open. The engine roared with power. When Joe popped the clutch, the Harley burned rubber and shot off through the underground garage.

Glancing in the rearview mirror, Joe watched the guards recede and finally disappear. He crossed the parking lot, then raced up a ramp to the street. Joe planned to ride in circles and then head for the outskirts of town to call Frank.

Frank. Joe was shocked at how he had accused his brother of being less than loyal. But how could Frank cautiously step back when a friend needed help?

The glaring headlights of a beat-up old Chevy flashed in Joe's rearview mirror. Joe made a right turn—the car followed. He sped up—so did the Chevy. Joe could see the shadowy forms of two men in the car's front seat.

"Enough of this playing around," he decided out loud, opening the throttle all the way and shifting into fourth. The bike whined and shot forward.

Joe was shocked to see the Chevy lurch forward and keep pace. Underneath that rusty, dented old body, he realized, was a fireball engine that exploded with power and speed.

Joe tapped the foot shifter into fifth, and the bike bolted forward. The car pounded along after the Harley. Joe crouched down to cut wind resistance. Even so, the Chevy caught up, bumping the bike's rear wheel. The cycle swerved, but Joe was able to maintain control.

How was he going to shake this tail? Joe realized he was near the railroad tracks. If he could keep the Chevy at bay for a few more minutes, he could zip down the embankment, hop onto the tracks, and follow them out of town. The car wouldn't be able to follow.

Joe heard a whine from the Chevy's engine. He turned to see the car leap forward and then felt it slam into the back of his cycle again. The bike pitched forward violently. Joe held on to the handlebars and kept himself from flipping off.

Now the cycle was weaving wildly down the street. Joe rode it out, steering into the erratic moves, going at high speed. He had almost regained control when the front tire struck a curb.

Moving at eighty miles an hour, the bike bucked like a wild bronco, unseating Joe and hurling him straight for a brick wall!

Chapter

5

FRANK DECIDED TO HEAD in the opposite direction from Joe. With luck, the security men would be too busy chasing Joe to get a good look at the van and its license number.

A hollow feeling settled in Frank's stomach—and it wasn't from hunger. It wasn't enough that the police were after Biker. Now they were probably after Frank and Joe as well. Then there was the way he and Joe had deliberately disobeyed their father. The law was one thing to have to answer to—Fenton Hardy was quite another.

"Joe once told me that whenever anybody needed help, Frank Hardy would be there." Biker's words cut through Frank's uneasy thoughts.

Frank glared at Biker in silence.

36

"He also said that when the odds were all against him, he wouldn't want anyone but you in his corner."

"Fine," Frank mumbled. "But he didn't have to be so eager to test it out."

"I *am* innocent, Frank."

"I know, but your attack on Brandon back there doesn't do much for your case."

"Oh, that." Biker laughed.

"Just like Joe," Frank said, "always too cool under pressure."

"I was trying to scare Brandon, not kill him," Biker went on. "He's a nice enough guy, but he has this habit of moving in on other people's girlfriends. Maybe things come too easy for him, since he's rich and handsome. If he doesn't watch himself, he can become the biggest jerk in the world.

"If his daddy didn't own the company, he would've been fired a long time ago, and I'd be vice-president in charge of sales."

"Why? He seems competent enough to me."

Biker laughed. "He tries too hard to be the boss. Once he came up with the brilliant idea of having all the field representatives call in at nine A.M., to make sure they were 'on the job.' Of course, as an executive, he wouldn't come in until ten, so his secretary handled the mess. Every morning at nine o'clock sharp, the company switchboard lit up like the Fourth of July—

then at one second past, the board would blow a fuse.''

"Why didn't Mr. Dalton stop it?''

"I tried to warn him, but he couldn't believe that anybody would have given such a stupid order. Then one day Mr. Dalton tried to call out at one second past nine and *zzzaaappp!*'' He laughed. "That day, Mr. Dalton was the one who blew a fuse.''

"What happened?" Frank asked as they turned down another street.

"Mr. Dalton got furious at Brandon. After that, Brandon made it tougher for me to route my shipments. I could handle that. But then he started getting personal by hitting on Sue. Just now, when I saw his cycle next to hers in the mall parking lot, I lost it.''

"Your temper just digs your hole deeper,'' Frank said.

"I've calmed down a lot since I met Sue.''

Frank frowned at Biker. He hadn't noticed any sign of a change.

"I can't believe you were convicted on such slim evidence,'' Frank said, his brow furrowed. "What could that truck driver have said to convince a jury?''

"If I get my hands on that liar, I'll choke the truth out of him!'' Biker slammed his fist against the dash. He looked out the window into the dark night. "Nick Frost testified that the hijacker was wearing black leather riding clothes exactly like mine, down to the emblems and logos I had sewn on from my junior motocross days. The only thing he couldn't see was my face—because of the racing mask."

"Racing mask?" Frank asked.

"Yeah. It looks like a ski mask, but it has one large oval for the eyes instead of two small holes."

"It still sounds like circumstantial evidence," Frank said.

"Frost claimed that he recognized the hijacker's voice as mine. I suppose he ought to know—I've chewed him out plenty of times for messing up my orders."

"Did you know Frost is missing now?"

"No."

Frank slowed the van to a halt.

"What's wrong, Frank?" Biker asked. He looked around, afraid that they had been stopped by the police.

"Nick Frost . . ." Frank said thoughtfully.

"What about him?"

"Each time I hear that name, a little bell rings." Frank hopped in the back of the van and unlocked the panel that held his laptop computer.

"Wow, High-tech Hardy," Biker said. "What are you trying to find in that little magic box?"

"A rat," Frank replied. A red light blinked on the computer and the screen jumped with amber letters. Moments later, Frank smiled for the first time in an hour. "And here he is, right in my dad's files. It seems Mr. Frost was once a petty crook here in Bayport, but hasn't been around for some time. How did you meet him?"

"Nick started working for DalTime about six months after I did. We drove together until I got promoted. He never said anything about being from Bayport."

"You wouldn't either if you had his record," Frank replied with a nod at the screen.

The data continued to scroll upward, listing Frost's past crimes. Biker whistled.

"Did he have anything against you?" Frank sat behind the steering wheel and started the van.

"The only time— Nah, that's silly."

"What?"

"About a year ago I got this great idea for promoting the watches and getting paid to ride cycles. Mr. Dalton let me form a company cycle club called Riding on Time. All of us—me, Sue, Brandon, Frost—would visit shopping centers and malls to put on safety and riding demonstrations. We had matching jumpsuits and—"

"What about Frost?" Frank said, interrupting the reminiscences.

"Brandon may be a jerk sometimes, but Frost makes stupidity an art form. The guy was careless, wouldn't follow instructions or stick to the routine. He nearly ran over some kids at one mall. Worse than that, he treated his bike like garbage. I finally told him to take a hike.''

Frank's eyes narrowed as he thought. ''So, Frost rides a bike?''

''Yeah, why?''

Frank described the attack at the pits. ''Joe said the guy's bike was a wreck.''

''Sounds like Frost. We used to joke that he never had to change his oil because it always leaked out first. He made a big fuss about being kicked out of our club but quieted down when Fat Harold's men started looking for him.''

''Fat Harold?''

''A loan shark with very long and very sharp teeth. From what I understand, Frost was deep in debt to Fat Harold and sinking fast.'' The van lurched from side to side as it hit several potholes. ''Hey, where are we going?''

''The computer gave Frost's last address. It's a garage owned by the Sinbads. If he's in town, he may be there.''

''The Sinbads?''

''They're a local cycle club known more for their fighting than their riding. I guess they were formed after you left Bayport.'' Frank turned down a dark street. ''Why would Frost be after you?''

''What do you mean?''

''Sue said that Frost disappeared shortly after you escaped. Did you threaten him at the trial?''

41

"I just looked at him," Biker said. "But you know what they say—if looks could kill . . ."

"Did you ever tell Frost about the pits?"

"I might have. Drivers talk about a million things on long hauls." Biker sat up. "Come to think of it, I did most of the talking."

Frank wasn't surprised.

He turned into a dark driveway. The van's headlights lit up the stained walls of a cinder-block garage. Rusted engine parts and skeletons of cycle frames cluttered the area. A large, poorly drawn picture of a skull with a blood-drenched knife between its teeth warned unwelcome visitors to stay away.

"Friendly folks, aren't they?" Biker mused.

Frank stopped the van several yards from the large wooden door of the seedy garage.

"Let me do the talking," Frank cautioned Biker, his hand on the door handle. "The last thing I need is for you to start a riot."

"Yes, sir," Biker said with a laugh and a salute.

Frank began to push open the door when it was suddenly jerked away from him. A large, hairy hand grabbed his shirt collar and yanked him out of the van. Then he was blinking in the glare of the headlights as a massive brass-knuckled fist flew toward his face. He had just enough time to move his head slightly. The brass knuckles only scraped along his jaw, but the force of the blow sent him stumbling backward.

A bearlike shadow was silhouetted against the headlights. The man swung his arm out and twisted his wrist. Frank heard the distinctive *snick* of a switchblade. A six-inch, razor-sharp blade glittered in the lights.

"My friends call me Switch." The huge man chuckled. "I usually keep this around in case of trouble. But when I heard you guys might be coming—I knew *I'd* be giving *you* trouble."

Chapter

6

JOE FLEW OFF the cycle, his fall cushioned by a pile of garbage. He rolled to one side as the bike slammed into the wall—hard. It fell to the ground, a hunk of twisted, screaming metal. The engine whined, then coughed, then died.

Joe lay quiet, the breath knocked out of him. He stayed still and took in small gulps of air. Revived, he tried to push himself up, but a burning line of pain shot down his left arm. Broken, he figured.

The Chevy screeched to a stop less than a yard from Joe, the headlight beams blinding him. He stood on wobbly legs. Although injured and dazed, Joe was ready to confront the two men getting out of the car. He wiped the grit and crud of the garbage from his visor and looked around, trying to find anything to use as a weapon.

The two men were still a blur. The driver leaned across the hood of the Chevy, pointing something at Joe. Joe instantly recognized the glint of steel from a large pistol.

"Okay, Conway," came a gravelly voice. "Back up to the wall." Joe had no choice as he heard the hammer lock into firing position. He backed up.

"Take the helmet off," the man ordered.

Joe tugged on the chin strap with his right hand. He loosened it and slowly pulled the helmet off his head.

"*Joe!*" Fenton Hardy yelled from the passenger side of the car.

Joe was momentarily confused. "Dad?" He caught himself as he began to fall forward.

Fenton ran to the front of the car and helped his son out of the garbage.

"What's going on here?" asked a puzzled Mort Sims. He still held his 9 mm on Joe, unsure what to do next.

"You've got the wrong guy, Sims," Joe said with a weak smile.

Sims lowered the hammer and replaced his gun in its holster.

"You've done it now, Fenton." He glared at Joe's father. "You told me that your sons were levelheaded, that they'd cooperate with the law.

I ought to arrest Joe here and now for aiding an escaped felon."

"What you'll do," Fenton replied harshly, eyes narrowed, "is drive Joe to the hospital."

Sims hesitated, then threw his hands up in the air and climbed into the driver's seat of the Chevy.

Joe cradled his left arm as Fenton helped him into the backseat.

"I think it's broken," he groaned.

"You're lucky you didn't break your neck," Sims retorted.

"Just drive, Sims," Fenton ordered as he hopped into the front passenger seat.

Reluctantly, Sims shifted the car and gunned the accelerator.

"What were you trying to prove by luring us away from Conway?" Fenton turned and asked after he gave Sims directions to the hospital.

"I wasn't luring you away from him." Joe tried to avoid his father's steel blue stare. "We didn't even know you were there. Biker got into some trouble at the mall, and I wanted to shake the security guards."

"Conway's a loser," Sims said matter-of-factly.

"Get off his back," Joe shot back.

"What kind of trouble?" Fenton Hardy wanted to know.

"Did you tell Brandon Dalton that Frank and I

46

were at the mall?'' Joe inquired instead of answering his father's question.

"He called the house about an hour after you left," Fenton answered. "He wanted to talk Biker into turning himself in."

"How'd he know to call our house?"

"I told him yesterday I was going to ask your father to help me," Sims replied. "Now, why don't you answer your father's questions?" Sims shot Joe a suspicious look.

"After we met Brandon and we talked a bit, he went to make a phone call. Next thing I knew, Biker was there and ready to punch him out."

"Was Murphy with Dalton?" asked Sims.

Joe hesitated. "Yes."

"So, Conway thought he'd do a little tap dancing on the guy who stole his girl." Sims laughed and turned to Fenton. "Word is that she dumped Conway for the rich kid after the trial."

"That's a lie," Joe said bluntly.

"Why didn't you call in, tell us where Conway was?" Fenton asked.

"Biker had just shown up when he got into the fight with Brandon."

"Where is he now?"

"With Frank."

"Where's Frank?" Sims asked impatiently.

"Driving around until Biker cools off."

"You were told to restrain him," Fenton said coldly.

"We had to get him away from the security guards," Joe replied. He knew what was coming the moment he said that.

"Why?" Fenton's voice was steady, like a flow of angry lava. "They would only have held him until the police arrived, and then Conway would have been put in jail—*where he belongs*."

"He's innocent," Joe protested. "If you'd really look at the evidence—"

"Judge Joe Hardy," Sims scoffed. "When's your appointment to the Supreme Court, Judge Joe?" Sims turned the car toward the hospital's emergency entrance. "You've got no reason to believe that Conway's innocent."

"My reason is based on something you wouldn't know much about," Joe said calmly.

"Yeah? What's that?"

"Friendship."

Joe watched in the rearview mirror as Sims's eyes narrowed into angry slits.

"You're lucky you *didn't* break that arm," the emergency room doctor said as he studied the X rays of Joe's left arm. "It's only a torn ligament—and a world-class bruise." He shut off the X-ray lamp and began writing on a chart. To a nurse he said, "Wrap it and put it in a sling." He turned to Joe. "You'll have to wear the sling for a few weeks. No baseball or tennis or anything that might agitate that arm.''

"Like helping escaped convicts," Sims added with a wry smile.

The doctor raised his eyebrows at Sims. "Just take it easy," he said, leaving the curtained room.

"I've known you for a long time, Fenton," Sims began as the nurse was adjusting the Velcro straps on Joe's sling. "You're one of the best investigators around. I never thought I'd be telling you this." Sims took a deep breath. "But if your boys get in my way again, I'll be forced to bring the law down on them. Hard."

Fenton's eyes bored into Sims. "My sons may have their faults. But breaking the law intentionally isn't one of them." Fenton approached the examining table where Joe was sitting. Joe was chilled by his father's icy stare. "Tell Sims everything you remember about Biker's old hangouts," Fenton ordered when the nurse left the cubicle.

Joe felt a great weight pull down on his shoulders. Fenton rarely used that tone of voice with either of his sons. Joe slid down from the table.

"You heard him," Sims said triumphantly. "Everything. I want that convict by morning."

Joe's mind was clear and calm. "No."

"I can't help you, Joe, if you insist on hampering Sims's investigation." Fenton Hardy's voice was no longer angry—just resigned to the fact that his son was sticking to his convictions.

"I won't betray an innocent friend to a trigger-happy bounty hunter like Sims." Joe paused. He felt the weight press down even more heavily. "Or to a bounty hunter like you."

Chapter 7

FRANK HARDY HEARD the sounds of a struggle from the other side of the van. But Biker would have to take care of himself—Frank had time only for the switchblade slicing toward him. He caught his attacker's arm as it swung down with the knife. Then Frank rolled, and Switch stumbled off balance. Whipping around, Frank snapped a kick behind the guy's left knee.

Switch grunted and fell to the ground.

Frank was on his feet in a flash. Switch rose slowly, the switchblade missing from his hand. Frank took a defensive karate stance. His teacher had taught him to let the bigger, more powerful guy make the first move, the first mistake.

A head taller and a foot thicker than Frank, the

bearlike man was slow. He swung a beefy fist at Frank. Frank slapped it away and moved back. Anger flashed in the man's eyes. He tried faking with his right and then jabbed with his left. Frank blocked the left jab and punched Switch in the nose. The man staggered back, shock and pain registering on his face. He snorted like a bull and charged Frank, his arms swinging in wide, wild arcs. Frank ducked and swiftly jammed his knee into the man's stomach. Switch doubled over but did not fall.

Frank decided to finish off the big man and help Biker. He moved toward the man for the knock-out punch. But Switch darted forward, catching Frank off guard. Two pile-driver gut punches had Frank wobbling on his feet. Then Switch threw a roundhouse right that connected right where the crowbar had hit Frank before.

Frank must have blacked out for a moment, because the next thing he knew, Switch had him in a bear hug. The man squeezed Frank just below the ribs and lifted him off the ground. Frank felt the air being forced from his lungs as Switch slowly tightened his grip. The big man knew the fight was already over. He was just ending it, the most painful way he knew.

Frank's lower ribs ached and his lungs screamed for air. He was too weak to kick, and his arms were pinned. Little pinpoints of light swirled behind his eyes—he was going to black out again. His head fell forward.

Switch chuckled a throaty, evil, triumphant laugh and shifted his grip.

When the arms around him loosened for a second, Frank snapped his head back, smashing it into the man's nose. Switch screamed and let Frank go, both hands going to his nose. The instant Frank's feet hit the ground, he spun and delivered a crunching kick to the man's jaw. Switch folded to the ground.

Frank stood over the thug, ready to deliver another blow if the man moved. His lungs felt as though a fire were raging inside as he took in short, choppy breaths. A dull ache rippled along his sore ribs. Switch remained still.

A steady rhythm of punches echoed from the other side of the van. Frank darted around the van, expecting to help Biker. Instead, he found Biker holding his assailant up, delivering quick jabs to the guy's face.

"Where is he?" Biker growled.

"D-d-d-don't . . . know," stammered the man.

Biker was set to deliver another set of blows when Frank shoved him back. Without Biker's support, the man crumpled to the ground.

"What are you doing, Frank? He would have told me where Frost is." Biker's eyes glowed with rage.

"If you didn't kill him first!"

Biker glared down at the man.

The roar of a motorcycle echoed in the air.

"The garage!" Biker shouted as he and Frank ran toward the cinder-block building.

The engine screamed high RPMs, and the cycle exploded out of the garage, shattering the old wooden door. A wood panel hit Biker and knocked him to the ground.

Frank found himself face-to-face with the cyclist—a tall, gaunt-faced guy with an old scar across his right cheek. The rider swerved his bike, kicking out and catching Frank on the hip. Frank tumbled backward.

"Frost!" Biker yelled, running into the garage.

Frank jumped to his feet.

A second cycle fired to life inside the cinder-block walls. The darkness of the night and the dust thrown up by Frost's escape hid what was happening. But Frank could figure it out.

"I'm going after Frost," Biker yelled as he downshifted. The cycle spat fire, and Biker shot off into the night in hot pursuit of Frost.

Frank rushed to the van and hopped in. He had to stop Biker before the wild man got hold of Frost. Frank knew that, given Biker's present state of mind, Frost's life was in danger.

Thanks to Joe's wizardry, the Hardys' black van was one of the hottest vehicles in Bayport. But Frank couldn't keep up with the two cycles. He slammed his fist against the dashboard as the red taillight of Biker's cycle disappeared into the dark. He jumped as the mobile phone chirped.

"What?" he bellowed into the phone.

"Hey, take it easy," said Joe.

"I've lost Biker."

"How?"

"We found Frost and got into a fight with a couple of those Sinbad creeps."

"What are you doing messing with the Sinbads?"

"I'll explain later. Where are you?"

"Home."

Frank sighed. "I'll be there in about ten minutes."

Frank found Joe in the kitchen where the younger Hardy was trying to manage an overstuffed sandwich with his one good hand.

"What happened to your arm?" Frank asked as he poured himself a glass of milk.

"Sims tried to run me down."

"What?"

"Dad was with him." Joe quickly explained about totaling Biker's cycle and refusing to give Sims any information. "I don't think I'll be asking Dad for any favors soon."

"I warned you about this," Frank said. He sat across from his brother.

"Don't give me that Frank Hardy I-told-you-so look." Joe raised the sandwich to his lips, only to have half the ham and pickles fall out the back. He put it down with a sigh.

"You really called Dad a bounty hunter?" Frank asked.

"Yeah."

"Where is he now?"

"Asleep. To calm Sims down, Dad had the police put out an all-points bulletin saying that Biker was dangerous and perhaps armed. Then he persuaded Sims to go back to his hotel and wait."

"You shouldn't have called Dad a bounty hunter."

Joe looked down at his mangled sandwich. "I know. I lost my temper. You'd think he would trust us. We would never do anything to hurt Dad."

"He knows that, but he's got Sims to deal with. I don't think it's a good idea to go sneaking behind Dad's back."

"We're not sneaking! We're helping a friend."

"Look, I believe Biker's innocent, too." Frank's voice rose. "I just don't want you putting your friend before the rest of the family." The shout strained Frank's bruised ribs. He winced, putting a hand to his side.

Joe sat back in his chair and stared at Frank. "What's wrong with your ribs?"

"A grizzly tried to squeeze me to death." Frank filled Joe in about the conversation in the van and the discovery that Frost was from Bayport. "I just hope Biker doesn't find Frost."

"Why?"

"I'm not sure if Biker's determined to prove himself innocent or if he just wants revenge. What if he knew Frost was from Bayport and came here looking for him? We could have been an afterthought." Frank glanced at the kitchen clock. "It's almost midnight. I ought to call Callie."

"Don't bother," Joe said as he pushed his sandwich away. "Brandon and Sue went back to their motel rooms, and Callie's at home." He paused. "Did Biker say anything about him and Sue and Brandon?"

"Just that Brandon had tried to move in on Sue."

"Sims claims that Sue's a gold digger, after Brandon for his money." Joe's lips twisted. "That guy's got some really wonderful ideas about people."

"He's just trying to rile you, Joe."

"Maybe it's working." Joe looked up at Frank. "Let's get some rest and start over in the morning."

Neither Frank nor Joe slept well. For both, the night passed slowly.

Frank's alarm awoke him from a restless sleep six hours later. He found Joe already up and in the living room waiting.

"Didn't you sleep?" Frank asked.

"Yeah. A little. You ready?" Joe asked as he zipped up a light fall jacket.

"Let me get some juice first," Frank protested.

Just then a loud thump echoed at the front door. Joe jumped.

"It's just the newspaper," Frank said. "Why don't you check out the headlines?"

Joe opened the door. Frank gasped.

Brandon Dalton swayed in the doorway, his boyish features swollen, bruised, and bloody. He stumbled, then caught himself. His eyes were wide with terror.

"Biker!" he whispered in a hoarse voice. "Biker."

He took a faltering step, trying to grab Frank. Then he fell to the floor in a heap.

Chapter

8

JOE GRIMACED AS he watched the nurse gently
rub gooey salve on a cut over Brandon's right
eye. Once Brandon was cleaned up, his face
didn't look so bad. He would have a swollen lip
and a black eye, but there were no serious inju-
ries.

Not wanting to wait for an ambulance, Frank
and Joe had rushed Brandon to Bayport Hospital
after he collapsed. Awakened by the disturbance,
Fenton had called Sims, and both men followed
the boys to the hospital.

"Well, it doesn't look as if anything's broken."
The emergency room doctor yawned as he
walked into Brandon's room. "However, I'd like

you to stay here for a couple of hours, just for observation.''

Brandon nodded weakly.

''Mind telling me what happened?'' Sims asked from a corner of the hospital room.

''All I wanted to do was talk Biker into turning himself in,'' Brandon said.

''Where did you find him?'' Frank asked.

''I didn't—he called me. Wanted me to meet him at the pits.''

''How do you know about the pits?'' Joe asked.

''Biker always talked about growing up in Bayport, being a junior motocross rider and all that drivel. He gave me directions to the quarry, and I met him there about four this morning. All he would say was that he had unfinished business from Mr. Pizza.''

''Mr. Pizza?'' Sims perked up.

''Biker and Brandon had a run-in there,'' Frank said quickly, ''but Biker was just trying to keep Brandon away from Sue.''

''I'd say he really finished the job.'' Sims tugged on his ear and nodded toward Brandon.

''We haven't heard Biker's side of the story and you've already got him convicted,'' Joe said hotly.

''His guilt should be obvious even to a junior detective,'' Sims sneered. ''First he breaks out of jail—that's real innocent. Then he tries twice to beat up on a friend who's trying to help him, just because he's jealous. The question is, why did he return to Bayport in the first place?''

"He wanted help," Joe replied.

"Yeah, right," Sims snorted. "Maybe he wanted to get rid of the only witness who put him behind bars.''

"That's crazy," Joe said with a glance at Frank.

His brother was silent, astonished that the bounty hunter was saying the same things he'd thought last night.

Sims puffed himself up and announced, "I'm bringing him in. I've never lost a bail jumper yet.''

"Just make sure Biker doesn't have any accidents before you get him back to New York," Joe warned.

"That depends on your friend." Sims smiled. "He can go back the easy way or the hard way. I don't judge people, you know. I just bring back fugitives. The courts decide whether they're guilty or innocent." His face hardened. "But nothing, especially two junior detectives, will stop me.''

Joe stepped forward, his fists clenched. He was ready to punch Sims when Fenton walked into the room. Joe froze, but Fenton stepped right past him. "Biker's been spotted," he announced.

"Where?" asked Frank.

"Just outside of town, near that old quarry.''

Frank gave Joe a sidelong glance.

Sims was out the door before Joe could stop him.

Noticing the concerned look on Joe's face, Fenton said, "I'll stick with him. If we catch Conway, he goes back to Queens with Sims."

Joe nodded silently.

"What are you two going to do?" Brandon asked from his hospital bed.

"We're going to try to find Biker before Sims does," Joe replied.

"I suggest we stay out of his way for the time being," Frank cautioned. "And I don't mean Sims's."

"Then what do we do? Sit around and twiddle our thumbs?" Joe was red with anger.

"I want to take another look at the Sinbads' garage," Frank said, ignoring Joe's outburst.

"That's a good idea," Brandon said. "I'll come with you." Brandon started to get up from his bed, but only fell back.

"You'd better stay here," Joe said. "The doctor said you could leave in a couple of hours."

"Yeah. You're right," said Brandon. "Call me if you find anything."

"Sure," Frank said. He nodded toward the door, and he and Joe left.

"Do you believe Biker beat up Brandon?" Joe asked as they neared the garage.

"I believe Biker is capable of doing just about anything if he gets angry enough."

Joe stared straight ahead. Biker *was* capable of losing his temper. Especially when he cared a lot about something—or some*one*, like a girlfriend.

Joe had seen Biker lose it completely three years earlier at a motocross event. Another cyclist had tried several times to kick Biker's cycle. Biker detested cheaters. After the race, Biker punched out the other rider and then took a hammer to the guy's motorcycle. When he was done, the cycle was totaled.

"Looks deserted," Frank said as he pulled the van to a stop and looked around.

Joe was too intent on looking at the run-down garage to hear Frank. He hopped from the van and scouted the area.

"It's clear," he said.

Frank shook his head. He'd have to keep an eye on Joe.

The door of the garage still lay in splinters where Frost had burst through. Frank and Joe entered the bay area and looked around. Frank tried a door leading to an office while Joe rummaged through some junk in the back.

The office wall was covered with motorcycle pictures and graffiti of skulls, cycle logos, and blood-drenched daggers. Frank cupped his hand over his nose—the office stank of decayed food. Something moved by the door—a large black rat. It squealed and scurried for the dark safety of a corner.

"You okay?" Joe yelled from the garage.

"Yeah," Frank replied. "Just introducing myself to one of the houseguests."

Joe was growing impatient. He kicked at the rubbish and boxes that lay about the bay area. He still didn't believe that Biker had deliberately lured Brandon out to the pits just to beat him up.

"Ow!" he yelled as his foot struck a wooden box hidden under a pile of dirty blankets. He looked closer, then threw the blankets aside. Stenciled on the side of the box was DalTime and a Queens address. Joe dug around in the blankets and discovered two more boxes. "Frank!"

"What's wrong?" Frank asked as he ran into the bay area.

"Got the time?" Joe smirked as he held up a handful of designer sports watches.

"Does anybody really know what time it is?" Frank replied, a wide grin on his face. For the first time in two days, he really began to believe that Joe had been right about Biker all along.

"This proves that Frost was in on the hijacking," Joe said.

"If the serial numbers match the invoice for the stolen watches," Frank replied.

"Why don't you just throw a wet blanket on the party?" Joe said sarcastically. Frank was being too cautious again.

"Look, Frost could have swiped these from any of the shipments he delivered."

Joe hated to admit it, but Frank was right.

"Let's take these three cases to Brandon. Maybe he can identify them," Frank said as he picked up one of the boxes.

Joe stacked the remaining box on the one he'd kicked and followed Frank out of the garage.

"Going somewhere?" a gruff voice asked.

Joe lowered his boxes. In front of Frank was a bearlike man, four other Sinbads at his side.

"Uh, how's business, Switch?" Frank tried to sound calm.

"Breaking and entering's a serious crime," Switch said with a chuckle. The big, burly biker seemed in a dangerously cheerful mood for a man whose nose was wrapped in bandages.

"Come on, Switch, let's quit fooling around. We've got to meet Frost at Daryl's," said a short, balding guy with an eye patch.

"Do what you want with old One-Arm here," Switch said, pointing at Joe's sling. He twisted his wrist and like magic his six-inch blade appeared.

"I've got some unfinished carving business with the other one."

Chapter

9

BRACING THEMSELVES BACK to back, Frank and Joe prepared for a hopeless fight. Frank knew that with his karate skills he could handle one of these guys, maybe two, but strength and numbers were on the Sinbads' side. And that didn't take into account the chains and clubs each Sinbad was holding.

Switch laughed and lunged carelessly at Frank. Frank moved to one side and delivered a smashing chop to Switch's wrist. The snap of bone and the cry of pain told Frank that Switch's knife hand was now useless.

Joe quickly decided that the best defense was a good offense. He yelled at two Sinbads as they approached. Surprised, the Sinbads hesitated.

Unable to use one arm, Joe charged, knocking both guys to the ground. But a third guy slugged Joe in the jaw, stunning the younger Hardy.

Frank saw Joe hit the ground. The Sinbad who had slugged Joe was raising a baseball bat over his head. With a spinning heel kick to the head, Frank sent that Sinbad to dreamland.

"Thanks," Joe said as he jumped to his feet.

"Any time," Frank replied.

"Kill 'em!" yelled Switch as he held his broken wrist, his face twisted in anger and pain.

The remaining Sinbads backed Frank and Joe against the garage wall. Clubs were raised and chains spun in the air. The two Hardys were in a fight for their lives.

A roar split the air. Behind the Sinbads, Frank and Joe could see a black-clad cyclist bearing down on the group.

"Biker!" Joe shouted.

The cyclist turned and braked the bike, ramming the three Sinbads. The bikers yelled as they flew into the air. The cyclist twisted the throttle handle and darted away.

Taking advantage of the confusion, Frank and Joe knocked the three guys out.

The cyclist rode up to Frank and Joe.

"Nice going, Biker," Joe said as the cyclist shut off the engine. Then the cyclist unstrapped the helmet and pulled it off. Joe was stunned. "What?"

Long auburn hair fell from beneath the helmet.

"Sue!" exclaimed Frank with a laugh.

"Glad I could help," Sue replied as she stepped from the Harley.

Callie pulled up in her car behind Sue and jumped out. "Surprise!"

"How did you know to find us here?" Frank asked as he put an arm around Callie.

"I called your house and found out about Brandon. Then I called the hospital to check on him," Sue replied. "He suggested that while you two were checking this place out, I should go back to Queens and look at Frost's apartment. I called Callie and asked if she wanted to come with me."

"And I suggested we meet here and tell you two," Callie added.

"I'm glad you did," Frank said with a smile.

"Where did you get that other cut?" Callie asked when she noticed the scrapes left by Switch's brass knuckles.

"From him," Frank said, pointing to the unconscious Switch. "We met here last night, too. This morning was round two."

"We found some evidence that will clear Biker," Joe said as he picked up one of the watch boxes.

"Great," Sue replied.

"It doesn't clear Biker yet," Frank said. "First we've got to prove that these are the watches that were stolen, and then that Frost actually hijacked the shipment.''

"You think Frost hijacked his own shipment and then framed Biker?'' Callie asked.

"Stranger things have happened,'' Frank replied.

"Frost hated Biker after he kicked him out of the company cycle club,'' Sue said thoughtfully.

"We'll explain later,'' Frank said in response to Callie's puzzled expression. "Let's tie up these clowns and try to find Dad.''

Callie called the police while Frank and Joe tied up Switch and his pals.

"Why did Brandon want you to check out Frost's apartment?'' Frank asked Sue.

"He's never believed that Biker stole those watches, and he thinks that maybe Frost had something to do with the hijacking.''

For the second time that day, Frank felt as though his mind were an open book.

"But why would Brandon send *you* to Queens? Why not Sims?'' Joe asked.

"I don't know,'' Sue replied with a shrug. "Brandon just said he was going back to the motel room to rest.''

"He's out of the hospital?'' Frank asked.

"Checked himself out,'' Sue responded. "He claimed the hospital was too noisy and he couldn't get any rest.''

"Did you hear him leave this morning when he went to meet Biker?"

"I heard a phone ring in the next room early this morning," Sue said. "It woke me up, but I was too sleepy to notice anything else."

"You didn't hear a cycle pull away?" Joe asked.

"I guess I went back to sleep," Sue said apologetically.

"She's not a sleuth like us," Callie said as she rejoined the group. "She doesn't distrust people the way we do."

Joe looked at Callie skeptically.

"Let's leave Callie's car and Sue's bike at the house," Frank suggested. "If we can't find Dad and Sims, we'll all go to Queens and search Frost's apartment."

While Callie looked for lunch stuff in the Hardys' kitchen, Frank tried to locate his dad and Sims. "No luck," he said to Joe.

"Don't you guys have anything besides fish sticks?" Callie yelled from the kitchen.

"No!" Frank shouted back. "Joe ate all the cold cuts last night."

"Brandon isn't answering his phone," Sue said as she returned from the den. She had tried to call Brandon on Fenton's private phone.

"He's gone?" asked Frank suspiciously.

"I doubt it," Sue replied. "He said the hospital

gave him a pretty strong sleeping pill and he was going to take a taxi back. He's probably out like a light.''

"You thinking that Brandon is involved in this somehow?'' Joe knew his brother well enough to read his thoughts.

"Why not?''

Sue laughed. "Brandon Dalton doesn't have the guts to say boo to his own shadow. He's all good looks and air.''

"Guess what?'' Callie said as she emerged from the kitchen. "You guys will have to buy us lunch along the way—unless you want fish-stick sandwiches.''

"We've got to get gas,'' Frank announced as they headed for the highway.

"Hey, remember what one of those Sinbads said to Switch?'' Joe suddenly asked with a start.

"What?''

"They were supposed to meet Frost at Daryl's. That's the gas station on Tenth.''

"That was a while ago,'' Callie pointed out.

"It's worth a try,'' Frank said as he turned the van down Tenth. "Maybe someone can tell us which way Frost went.''

Daryl's was one of the last full-service stations left in Bayport.

"Why are you stopping here?'' Callie asked as

Frank pulled the van into a vacant lot across the street from Daryl's.

"Look." Frank pointed to a Harley parked by the gas pumps.

"Let's check it out." Joe hopped from the van before Frank could say anything.

"Wait here," Frank said to Callie and Sue. "That might not be Frost's bike."

Joe was kneeling beside the bike when Frank approached.

"Ever seen an oil leak like that?" Joe asked. Directly beneath the engine was a dirty black patch of oil.

"Must have been here awhile," Frank noted, "to leak that much oil."

"Not so long," Joe said. "The tank isn't filled yet." The nozzle was in the bike's gas tank, and the pump was still working.

"Can I help you guys?"

Frank and Joe spun round. The station attendant leaned against the doorway leading into the office, wiping his greasy hands on an even greasier T-shirt. Joe recognized him from school.

"Hey, Randy," he said with a friendly wave. "Know whose bike this is?"

"No." Randy walked over to Frank and Joe.

"Know where the guy is?" Frank asked.

"Why?"

"I've been looking for a bike like that." Joe forced a smile.

"That piece of junk! I thought you knew something about bikes," Randy scoffed.

Joe sighed. "Just tell us where he is."

Randy shrugged. "Guy said he was going to the bathroom." He turned and wandered back inside the office.

"I'll check around the side," Joe said. "Try to phone Dad. Maybe he's—"

Joe's last words were cut short by the blast of a gun. The bullet smashed glass on the pump next to Joe. Frank and Joe jumped behind the pumps.

"Where'd that come from?" Frank yelled.

"Over there!"

Frank followed Joe's pointing finger. A small-barrel .38 was sticking out around the edge of the building, held by someone wearing a black cycle helmet.

"What's going on out—" Randy began as he stepped outside the station office.

"Get back!" Joe shouted and jumped up, waving the attendant back.

Frank yanked Joe back down as the gunman fired again.

Two more shots quickly followed. The last bullet struck the gas hose leading to Frost's Harley. The rubber hose split in two and fell to the ground. Gas spread around the cycle and the island.

"The gas pump!" Frank yelled.

Joe reached over to shut off the pump, but

before he could, a fourth shot rang out. The bullet hit the concrete, sending sparks in all directions and hitting the rapidly spreading pool of gas. The gas exploded.

In a fraction of a second, the entire island of pumps was enshrouded in bright blue flames— with Frank and Joe caught in the middle!

Chapter

10

"WE'RE SURROUNDED!" Joe yelled as he held up his arms to protect his face from the flames.

A thick black plume of smoke rose into the air like a dark mushroom.

Frank spun around. Joe was right. Flames encircled them. Worse yet, the flames were getting thicker as more gas ran out. Running through the flames would mean getting seriously burned. But staying there would ensure a horrible death.

"The pump's going to explode!" Joe stared in horror as the fire ran up the split hose and engulfed the pump.

Frank spotted their one chance to escape.

"Over here, Joe!" he yelled above the crackle of the fire. He grabbed the faucet of the island's water hose and twisted it open. There was no way water could put out a gasoline fire, but . . . he held the hose over his head until he was completely soaked; then he turned it on Joe. "Ready?"

"Yeah," Joe replied.

"One, two, *three*."

The Hardys threw themselves into the flames and emerged singed but safe seconds later. Simultaneously, they rolled on the ground to smother any flames. Callie and Sue covered them with their jackets.

"You okay?" Joe asked as he brushed himself off.

Frank nodded.

Screams sounded from inside the station's office.

"Randy!" Joe yelled. "He'll be trapped inside."

Frank turned—to find Callie dashing into the small building. She grabbed the terrified attendant by the arm and tried to pull him toward the door. But Randy was crazy with fear. As Frank burst through the door, Randy's terrified thrashing had sent Callie spinning into a candy machine. She hit hard, gasped, and slid to the floor. Frank helped her up, grabbed the attendant, and began pulling him toward the door.

A sudden rush of air and heat hit Frank. He jumped back, watching helplessly as a wall of gas-fed flames rose up to block their only exit.

"We're gonna die!" the attendant screamed as he pulled away from Frank and ran to a corner of the office.

Frank grabbed a chair and threw it into the picture window on the side of the building. He dragged the attendant from the corner and hurled him out, sending him staggering to safety. Callie wobbled to her feet. Frank put his arm around her and both scrambled through the broken window.

Joe rushed forward to grab the dazed attendant. All four sprinted away from the building.

A loud crack shattered the air as the pumps exploded. The concussion and blast slammed them all to the ground. Thick black smoke rolled over them and began to choke them. Frank and Callie crawled away from the smoke as Joe and Sue dragged Randy away from danger.

Seconds later the gas station was surrounded by fire engines, police cars, and ambulances. Half an hour later the fire was extinguished, leaving the station a charred skeleton.

"Are you boys okay?" asked Officer Con Riley with concern. He had arrived with the fire engines and had waited till the paramedics had checked Frank, Joe, and Callie over.

"Yes," Frank replied. "But I don't think I'll want to roast hot dogs anytime soon."

"Mind telling me what happened here?" Officer Riley asked.

Frank hesitated, then explained that he, Joe, Callie, and Sue had been looking for Frost when they spotted his cycle at the gas station. "Next thing we knew, someone was shooting at us," Frank finished his story.

"And you think it was Frost firing at you?" Con asked.

"Yes," Joe said without hesitation. "We had a run-in with some members of his gang earlier. He knew we were on his tail."

"Hey, Con, come over here and look at this!" a fire fighter yelled as he pointed into a ditch next to the station.

"You four stick around. I'm not through getting your statements," Con Riley said as he walked toward the fire fighter.

"Shouldn't we tell him about the watches you and Frank found at the Sinbads' garage?" Sue asked Joe.

"Not yet," Joe replied. "The watches by themselves don't prove Frost was in on the hijacking. We need to check out Frost's apartment first."

"Frank, Joe, come over here," Officer Riley shouted.

Frank and Joe walked over to the ditch.

"Know who he was?" Officer Riley asked, pointing into the ditch.

They saw the body of a dead man with a switchblade in his back. On his left forearm was a tattoo of a snowflake with a blood-drenched knife sticking through it. But Frank stared at the gaunt, scarred face.

"It's Nick Frost, isn't it?" Frank asked.

"Right you are," Con replied. "Know how he got here?"

"No," Joe said quickly.

"I guess someone else must have been shooting at you two," said Con Riley. He walked down into the ditch and knelt beside the body. "What's this?" he asked, pulling a wallet from beneath the body. He opened it, took out a driver's license, and then stood. "You two know somebody named Robert Conway?"

Frank and Joe looked at each other with stunned expressions.

"He's a friend of ours," Frank finally said.

Officer Riley signaled for Randy to join them, then gestured at Frost's body. "Is this the man who came in to get gas?" he asked the attendant.

"Y-yes," Randy answered. His face went pale when he looked at the dead man.

"See anybody else?"

"Another guy on a bike pulled up after he did," the attendant replied.

"What did he look like?" Joe asked. He glanced at Con Riley, who didn't appreciate Joe's butting in.

"I couldn't tell. He had on a black helmet and a black leather motorcycle jacket and pants."

The attendant looked at Con Riley. "Can I go now? I think I'm going to be sick."

Officer Riley nodded, and the attendant hurried away.

"Conway," Con Riley said thoughtfully. "I arrested him about three years ago for buying stolen motorcycle parts. He's an escaped con, isn't he?"

"He's as innocent now as he was three years ago," Joe rapped out.

Officer Riley, tapping the license against his hand, looked skeptically at Joe. "The description we have at the station says he rides a new Harley."

"His bike was destroyed when it smashed into a brick wall," Joe said.

"How would you know that?" Riley asked, his eyes full of suspicion.

Joe raised his injured arm in its sling. "I was on it at the time."

"What about the bike he took from the Sinbads?" Callie asked.

"Callie!" Joe shouted. He couldn't believe that Frank's girlfriend would betray Biker.

Frank quickly explained to Con Riley about the first run-in with the Sinbads the night before. "But Biker wasn't wearing his helmet or his jacket," he concluded.

"That's right," Joe added. "*I* have them. They're still in the van." Joe rushed over to the van, pulled out Biker's helmet and jacket, and handed them to Con.

"There's no proof that these are Conway's," Riley said.

"You have my word they are," Joe told him.

Con Riley looked at the jacket and helmet and then at Joe. "This may cost me my badge, but I believe you. It still doesn't clear Conway, though."

"Look at this," Frank said from the ditch.

Joe and Officer Riley joined Frank, who was holding up one of Frost's hands.

"Frost's knuckles are scraped and bruised, as if he'd been in a fight," Frank said.

"You're right," Riley replied. "But I don't see why that's important."

"*Look* at him," Frank said.

Joe and Con Riley looked at Frost's unbruised face.

"If he'd been in a fight, he should be all marked up, shouldn't be? There's not a cut on him."

Con Riley tilted back his hat and scratched his head.

Just then, Sims's beat-up old Chevy pulled up next to the police cars. Sims and Fenton Hardy got out and walked over to the ditch.

"Nick Frost," Frank explained when his father stood beside him.

"Any suspects?" Fenton asked Con Riley.

"The attendant said that another cyclist pulled

up shortly after Frost. That was the last he saw of Frost or the other guy.''

"Whoever killed Frost tried to kill us, too," Frank added.

"Conway," Sims growled.

"What?" Joe demanded angrily.

"With Frost gone, Conway has a better chance of having his conviction overturned," Sims replied.

"He wouldn't shoot at us," Joe said through clenched teeth.

"Your friend's a convicted thief. I've dealt with scum like him before. You can't trust him."

"We've got proof that Biker didn't steal those watches!" Joe blurted out.

His words were drowned out as a police radio blared a report. "Suspect apprehended at edge of town."

A triumphant grin spread across Sims's face as he grabbed Biker's license from Con Riley.

"It doesn't matter whether he stole the watches or not. He's a murderer—and now he's locked up."

Chapter

11

"I WANT TO SEE Biker and hear his side of the story," Joe demanded.

"Forget it, kid," Sims replied.

"It's best that you stay away from Conway," Fenton agreed.

"Your father's right," Sims went on. "You shouldn't be hanging around a killer."

"He's not a murderer!" Joe shouted. He lunged at Sims, grabbing the older man by the lapels of his jacket. Frank pulled his brother away.

"Settle down," Frank said. "You're not doing Biker any good by losing your temper."

Frank had to drag Joe over to the van, out of Sims's hearing.

"Look, Biker's safe in jail," Frank whispered harshly. "Whoever killed Frost and shot at us will probably try to get Biker, too. Anybody desperate enough to kill once won't hesitate to do it again."

Frank was relieved to see a glint of understanding come into Joe's eyes. "Now, let's go to Queens and search Frost's apartment before Sims gets the idea to do the same thing."

Joe nodded and climbed into the passenger side of the van.

"You still want to come along?" Frank asked Sue.

"Staying here won't help Biker," she replied. "Besides, you'll be able to find Frost's apartment more quickly with me to guide you."

With that, Frank, Callie, and Sue got into the van.

"Where are you going?" Joe asked as Frank pulled away from the burnt gas station. "The highway to New York is in the other direction."

"I know," Frank replied. "I don't want Sims to see us leaving town. So I'll head downtown for a couple of blocks and then take another route to the highway." Frank checked his rearview mirror several times to make sure Sims wasn't following.

"This is it," Sue said a couple of hours later.

Frank stopped the van in front of a dingy five-story apartment building.

"Frost's place is on the third floor," she added, "apartment three-F."

"You two keep watch outside," Joe said as he hopped into the back of the van and opened a box containing various disguises. "Frank and I will handle this."

Callie was ready to protest when Frank raised his hand.

"We'll need some warning if Sims or the cops show up," he explained, then winked at Callie.

Callie smiled as she and Sue got out of the van.

"Acme Speedy Delivery," Joe said as he threw one of two blue jumpsuits at Frank.

They quickly pulled on their disguises. Joe grabbed a clipboard and handed a wrapped, empty box to Frank.

"That ought to do it," he said.

The inside of the apartment building was as dingy as the outside. Frank and Joe had to use the stairs because the elevator had broken down.

"Here it is," Joe said as they walked down a darkened hallway.

Frank put the box on the floor and pulled out a case full of lock picks. He crouched down, inserted a pick in the lock, and in seconds had opened the door.

They entered the apartment and Frank locked the door from the inside.

"This place could stand a tidal wave of disinfectant," Frank said, wrinkling his nose at the smell of dirty laundry and unwashed dishes.

Joe was too busy going through Frost's dresser drawers to notice the smell.

Frank walked over to a window and opened it to air out the room. He looked around. The place was a mess. Food wrappers, dirty TV-dinner trays, old clothes, cycle magazines, and record albums littered the floor. Frank kicked some of the stuff out of his way and decided to check under the bed.

Joe took everything out of the drawers but found no clues. He pulled the drawers out to check the bottoms and back. Still nothing. He moved the dresser away from the wall. When he found nothing again, he pushed the dresser over in frustration. It hit the floor with a crash and Frank jumped up.

Then came a pounding on the wall.

"Hey, knock it off in there. I'm trying to sleep," yelled a rough voice.

"Take it easy, Joe," Frank said. "If there's something here, we'll find it."

Joe headed for the closet. He kicked a stack of magazines out of his way. The magazines scattered, several landing next to Frank. He shook his head and looked down. Sticking out of one was an envelope. He pulled it out of the magazine and smiled. Printed on the front of the envelope was the DalTime company logo. Beneath it was Frost's name.

Frank was about to call out to Joe when he heard the distinctive metal click of a gun's hammer. He turned. A large, burly man was climbing through the open apartment window from the fire escape, a steel blue .45 automatic in his hand.

"We've got company, Joe," Frank said quietly.

Joe spun around. Two more men came in the window; the second looked just as big and mean as the first and held a twin to the first man's .45. The third man was small, thin, and pale. His pig-eyes were deep-set and small.

"Gentlemen," the thin man said in a tinny, high-pitched voice, with all the charm of a cobra, "making a special delivery?"

"We were just leaving," Frank said quickly. He turned to leave, hoping none of the men saw him tuck the envelope into his jumpsuit.

The first man moved to the door and leveled his .45 at Frank's chest. Frank noted the gunman's casual, businesslike expression.

"It's rude, just running off and leaving your guests," the small man said. His thin-lipped smile stretched from cheek to cheek.

"Hey, man," Joe said, "we got about ten more deliveries before we can knock off work. I don't want to miss the big game on the tube tonight."

The thin man's expression hardened. He nodded, and the second thug moved to the other side of Joe, his .45 aimed at Joe's stomach. The two thugs now flanked the Hardys.

"Gentlemen, I'd like you to meet Mr. Rock," the thin man said with a nod to the thug next to Frank. "And this is Mr. Hard Place," he added with a nod to the thug next to Joe. "You two must be Mr. Stuck and Mr. Between."

The thin man laughed, his high-pitched giggles echoing in the room. "Get it? Stuck between a rock and a hard place?"

"Real funny," Frank shot back. "My partner wasn't kidding. We could get fired if we don't—"

"*Shut up,*" the thin man growled. He walked over to Frank. "You look very familiar to me," he said. "Have we met before?"

"No," Frank replied coolly.

"Let me introduce myself. I'm Fat Harold." The thin man was visibly disappointed that neither Frank nor Joe seemed to recognize his name.

"*Fat* Harold?" Joe said in disbelief. "A weed like you couldn't get wet running around in the shower."

Fat Harold laughed. Frank grimaced at the grating giggle.

"*This* is why they call me Fat Harold." The man reached into his pocket and pulled out a two-inch-thick wad of folded bills. He began flipping the bills as though he were counting them.

Frank's and Joe's eyes widened—all the bills were hundreds.

"You're a bookie," Frank stated.

"Very good, kid," Fat Harold said with a smile as he put the money back into his pocket. "And you're no delivery men."

"Should I kill them now, Mr. Harold?" Rock asked.

Although the question startled Frank, it was the thug's calm tone that disturbed him most. Rock sounded as if he had asked about ordering a pizza.

"No, I don't think that will be necessary," Fat Harold replied. "It's obvious that these two are looking for the same person we are. You see, boys, my *pocket change* is actually a little short this week, thanks to a thief named Biker Bob Conway."

Frank and Joe glanced at each other.

"Ah, so you know the little welsher. Good. What's he into you for?"

Joe stared at him, confused.

"About ten grand," Frank answered quickly, realizing that Fat Harold was assuming he and Joe were bookies also.

"Petty cash." Fat Harold was unimpressed. "Conway owed me nearly a quarter of a million in bad debts."

"Owed?" Frank asked.

"He missed his last payment deadline when they caught him with the watches."

"Watches?"

"Yeah. Some harebrained scheme of his to pay me two hundred and fifty grand by stealing some watches from the company he worked for," Fat Harold explained. "I didn't get my money or my watches."

"Why did you think he'd be here?" Frank asked.

"I got a call from a little birdie about an hour ago saying Conway would be here," Fat Harold replied. He stared suspiciously at Frank. "What brings you two to these lovely surroundings?"

"Uh, we knew Frost and Conway were friends and thought we'd find one of them here, get our dough," Frank said quickly.

"What happens now?" Joe asked.

"Now I'll take Conway in nice little pieces," Fat Harold said slowly. "It'll be worth a ten percent finder's fee for you two boys if you find him and give me a call."

"Sounds great," Frank said.

"Here's my card."

Frank looked at the business card Fat Harold handed him. No address or name—just a distinctive number: 555-BETS.

"Cool," Frank said. He stuck the card in his back pocket.

Fat Harold stared at Frank's face again. "Are you sure we haven't met before?"

"Positive," Frank answered.

"I don't know," Fat Harold said thoughtfully. "Something about you . . . Rock, check his ID."

Frank stepped back to confront Rock, but froze when the big man stuck the .45 against his chest. Rock pulled Frank's wallet from his back pocket and flipped it open.

"His name is Frank Hardy," Rock said, handing the wallet back to Frank.

"Frank Hardy," Fat Harold said slowly. He walked across the room to the window, rubbing his chin in thought. He snapped his fingers. *"Hardy!* That's who you look like."

Fat Harold stared at Frank's face. "When I first started out in this business, an NYPD detective named Fenton Hardy made my life miserable. He was the only cop who ever put me in jail." Fat Harold walked around Frank. "Yeah, you look like a younger Fenton Hardy." Fat Harold's voice began to sound amused. "Maybe like his son!"

"Hey, man," Joe said. He stepped toward Fat Harold, only to be shoved back by the barrel of Hard Place's .45.

Fat Harold held out his hand, and his thug handed over Joe's wallet. "Another Hardy, huh?" Fat Harold's nasal laugh echoed in the room. "The sons of Fenton Hardy. You almost had me believing you were bookies."

His expression became cold, hard, deadly. "Kill them." The bookie's voice sounded almost bored as he turned and headed for the window.

"Yes, sir, Mr. Harold," Rock replied.

After he had exited through the window, Fat Harold leaned back in from the fire escape and said, "Rock, make sure you get my business card back. Nothing personal in this, boys. We're just settling an old debt. I spent two years in prison because of Fenton Hardy. Two years for two sons. Sounds fair."

His laugh bounced off the walls in the alley as he climbed down the fire escape.

"Let's have the card," Rock ordered. Frank took it from his pocket and flipped it at Rock.

"Stand over there," Rock ordered with a wave of his gun. "Lace your fingers behind your heads."

Frank and Joe moved toward the center of the room, hands behind their heads. Both were looking for an opportunity to escape, but Rock stood behind them and Hard Place in front.

"Like Mr. Harold said," Rock began as he walked around in front of Frank and Joe, "nothing personal. We're just doing our jobs. Kneel down."

Just a job, Frank thought. If not for the guns,

Rock and Hard Place would look as if they were taking orders behind the counter at Mr. Pizza.

The two thugs slipped six-inch silencers from their pockets and screwed them onto their pistols. They checked their safeties and locked the hammers into firing position.

Frank and Joe glanced at each other. They'd always expected to go out with a bang.

Instead, they'd go out with a whisper—shot in a gangland-style execution by the silenced guns of two bored killers.

Chapter

12

ROCK'S HEAD JERKED up as someone began banging loudly on the door.

"Hey! Open up! We know you two deadbeats are in there!" An angry voice shrilled from the other side of the door. It was Callie, yelling as loud as she could.

"Yeah. You're not getting away this time," Sue shouted through the door. "We want those paychecks before you gamble them all away!"

"Who's that?" Rock asked Frank.

"How should I know?" Frank replied sharply.

The pounding on the door grew louder.

"Knock off that noise!" someone yelled from another apartment.

"You tell those good-for-nothing husbands of ours to come out now!" Callie yelled.

"Yeah," Sue added. "They're not wasting their paychecks on card games this time!"

"Go away," Rock yelled back. "You got the wrong place."

The pounding continued. Somewhere down the hall a baby screamed itself awake and began crying loudly.

"Let's do it and get out of here," Hard Place said, nervousness showing in his voice.

Joe knew it was the right moment to make his move. Hard Place glanced over at Rock for a split second, and that was enough time for Joe to slam a steel fist into the thug's gut. Hard Place gagged and doubled over.

Frank grabbed one of the drawers Joe had taken out of the dresser and threw it at Rock. The drawer cracked against Rock's skull and shattered into tiny pieces.

Like twin bolts of lightning, Frank and Joe dashed for the open window. They scrambled down the metal steps and then jumped from the fire escape ladder and hit the asphalt pavement of the alley in a dead run toward the street.

A second later they heard the *phfft, phfft, phfft* of .45 slugs slamming into the ground behind them.

The Hardys' black van screeched to a halt at the end of the alley.

"Hurry!" Callie yelled from the front seat.

The side door of the van slid open. Sue waved frantically for Frank and Joe to run faster.

"Step on it!" Frank yelled as he and Joe leapt into the van.

Callie mashed the accelerator to the floor, sending Frank, Joe, and Sue tumbling around the back of the van. She turned the first corner and gunned the engine again.

"Slow down!" Joe shouted after several more two-wheel turns.

Callie stomped on the brake and Joe lurched toward the front of the van and fell forward against the dash. His injured arm smacked into the mobile phone, breaking it.

Joe let out a yell of anguish, cradling his arm. "I felt safer back there with those two thugs than I do with you."

"Oh, yeah?" Callie fumed. "Maybe you'd like me to take you back there."

"Crazy girl driver," Joe shouted back.

"Knock it off, you two!" Frank was in no mood for one of Joe and Callie's famous fights. "Let's get out of here before they catch up with us."

Joe jumped into the passenger seat and buckled his seat belt.

"Ready," he said.

Callie huffed in exasperation, put the van into drive, and started forward at a normal pace.

"The least you could do is say thanks," Sue said from the back of the van. "Something terrible could have happened to you two if we hadn't thought so quickly."

Joe remained silent.

"How did you know we were in trouble?" Frank asked.

"Callie asked me to check out the alley. I spotted Fat Harold and his two bodyguards climbing up the fire escape. I called Callie over, and when she saw Fat Harold leave without his goons, she knew you two needed help and came up with the idea of pretending to be your wives. She's a real hero."

"How do you know Fat Harold?" Frank asked.

"He came around the company a few times, looking for Nick Frost. Mr. Dalton, Brandon's father, had to call security to run him off. Fat Harold's a real pain in the neck."

"Does he know Biker?" Joe asked.

"Only Biker's shoes." Sue laughed. "Biker almost took his head off one day at work," she explained. "We were walking out to the car, and Fat Harold was hanging around waiting for Frost. He whistled and made a rude remark to me. Biker took out Fat Harold's two bodyguards first and then started for Fat Harold. That guy is so thin that when he saw Biker heading for him, he crawled under his limousine and refused to come out till Biker left."

"Did Biker owe Fat Harold any money?" Joe wanted to know.

"No."

"According to Fat Harold, Biker owes him two hundred fifty thousand dollars in gambling debts."

"That's impossible," Sue protested. "Frost was the only one at the company who placed bets with Fat Harold."

"Then why did Fat Harold say he was looking for Biker?" Joe said more to himself than to the others. "I wish we'd found something to help us make some sense of all this."

"Maybe we have." Frank pulled the DalTime envelope from his pocket.

"What's that?" Joe said, excitement in his voice.

"Let's find out." Frank ripped open the envelope, pulled out several sheets of paper, and scanned them.

"Well?" Joe was impatient.

"What do you make of these?" Frank handed the papers to Sue.

She took the papers and glanced through them.

"What are they?" Joe asked, unbuckling his seat belt and joining Sue and Frank in the back of the van.

"We have something here." Sue held up the first sheet. "This is a shipping invoice and schedule for three hundred cases of Watch Ya Wearing?

watches to a large retail store chain in Kansas City. And"—she held up the second sheet—"this is a schedule of employee vacations with Biker's name underlined in red."

"And this," Frank said, holding up a third sheet, "is a road map with a major highway leading out of Queens and New York City outlined in red."

"So what does all this prove?" Callie asked.

Joe's attention was on Sue. "Did Frost have access to shipping invoices?"

"Only for the deliveries he made." Then she added, "But he had no business with the vacation schedules. Those are supposed to be confidential."

Joe noticed a look of disappointment come over Frank's face. "What's wrong?"

"The marks on this map end somewhere in northern New Jersey—on a highway in the middle of nowhere. There's March thirtieth and an *X* marked, and above that is 'B—seven-thirty.' " He looked grim. *"B* for Biker."

"March thirtieth at seven-thirty! That's when the hijacking took place, according to Frost's testimony," Sue said.

"Where was Biker on that date?" Joe asked Sue.

"He'd just returned from his cross-country vacation. He got to my place at about eight, and we went out for dinner at eight-thirty."

"The spot where the truck was hijacked is a good thirty miles away," Frank said. "Biker couldn't have hijacked the truck, hidden it, and then gotten to your house by eight. Didn't his lawyer point that out to the jury?"

"Yes, but the prosecutor said that as an expert driver and a former motocross champion, Biker had the skill to just make it to my house from the highway."

"That stinks," Joe objected. "For all we know, that *B* could stand for 'Plan B' or Boise, Idaho. Frost hijacked his own truck. Let's just go back to Bayport and prove it."

"We can't do that just yet," Frank said.

"Why not?"

Frank ignored Joe's angry question and turned to Sue. "Could Frost access the vacation schedule from any of the company's computers?"

Sue shook her head. "Frost was a little slow. On his good days, he could barely remember his own address, much less try to figure out how to use a computer."

"Then somebody must have given him the information—somebody who knows the company's computer access codes and who needed half a million bucks' worth of designer watches." Frank stared at Sue.

She looked at him. "The only one who was in any sort of trouble was Frost."

"And his troubles are over now," Callie reminded them from the front seat.

"What are these numbers up here?" Frank asked as he pointed to the top of the shipping invoice.

"Sales rep's code number and shipping date," Sue replied.

Frank looked at the invoice sheet and then at the vacation schedule. A wide grin came across his face.

"What is it?" Joe asked.

"I'm not sure," Frank replied. He faced Sue. "I'll need to get into your company's computers and check something out first. Can we get in there without too many people finding out?"

Sue looked at her watch. "By the time we get to the offices, almost everybody should be gone for the day. But the security guards won't stop me from showing my cousins around," she added with a smile. "Problem is, we'll have to double back the way we came. Suppose Fat Harold is there and recognizes the van?"

"No problem," Frank said, heading for the van's storage space. "We've got a bag full of tricks back here."

Callie pulled the van into a vacant parking lot. Fifteen minutes later, plastic signs on both sides of the van advertised the Bug-B-Gone exterminating company. Atop the van was a four-foot-long black-and-orange inflatable bug, held securely to the van's roof by magnetic feet.

"That thing sure is ugly," Callie said as she looked at the bug through the van's sun roof.

"Yeah, but those two thugs are looking for an Acme Speedy Delivery van," Frank said.

"Don't you think the bug makes us a little too obvious?" Sue asked.

Frank smiled. "Sometimes the best place to hide is in plain sight. Okay, Sue. Which way?"

The watch company was near the Queens-Brooklyn line in an old factory building that was being renovated. Frank was glad to see that the employee parking lot was nearly empty.

"Don't turn the light on," Frank said as they entered Sue's second-floor office. "I don't want to attract any attention."

Sue sat at her desk and booted up her computer. She typed in several security access codes. "It's all yours, Frank."

Frank took Sue's place at the terminal. He typed in the sales rep's code and Biker's Social Security number.

"Where's that door lead?" Joe asked, pointing to a large wooden door opposite Sue's desk.

"That's Mr. Dalton's office," Sue replied.

"What are you looking for?" Callie asked Frank impatiently.

"I'll let you know when I find it," Frank replied absently. He was looking for a microneedle in a computer haystack, and he didn't need any distractions.

Joe paced the small office. Biker was sitting in jail facing an assault charge for beating up Brandon and a murder charge for the death of Frost, and two hoodlums working for a small-time bookie were gunning for Biker, Frank, and Joe. The last two days hadn't been shining ones for the Hardys.

"Yeah!" Frank announced triumphantly.

"What is it?" Joe rushed around the desk and stared at the display terminal. The letters and numbers on the screen meant nothing to him. "Would you mind explaining this to me?"

Before Frank could answer, the door across from Sue's desk creaked open.

Joe turned—just in time to stare into the black eyes of a Doberman springing over the desk toward him, its sharp teeth aiming right for Joe's throat.

Chapter

13

"JOE!" FRANK YELLED as he tossed a ruler to his younger brother.

Joe caught the ruler and smacked the Doberman on the nose. The dog fell to one side, sneezed, shook its head, and crouched to spring again.

"Sit, Trooper!" yelled Sue.

The black Doberman sat down and growled at Joe, exposing large yellow teeth.

"This is *your* dog?" Joe asked Sue, keeping his eyes on the Doberman and the ruler ready to smack the dog again.

"He's the company's dog," answered a silver-haired man from the open doorway.

"Mr. Dalton," Sue gasped.

"Sue," Mr. Dalton answered in a surprised yet relieved voice. "What are you doing here? Who are these people?"

"Frank, Joe, Callie," Sue said, "this is Scott Dalton, founder and president of DalTime, Inc."

"Brandon's father?" Callie asked.

"Looks that way," Joe muttered.

"Why are you here? I thought you were looking for Biker," Mr. Dalton said.

"Frank and Joe are detectives from Bayport," Sue explained. "Biker asked them to help him. We came here looking for evidence that might prove Biker's innocence."

Joe moved toward Mr. Dalton and was about to explain why they had sneaked into the offices when Trooper stood up and growled.

"Out, Trooper," Mr. Dalton ordered, a deep scowl on his face. The black Doberman gave a small whine and meekly left the room. "Sorry about the dog, Joe," Mr. Dalton said. "I got him shortly after the trial, when the phone calls started."

"What phone calls?" Joe asked.

"Someone began threatening to hurt me. Although the voice was disguised, I thought it was Biker." Mr. Dalton sat in a chair opposite Sue's desk. Frank could read the weariness and worry on the older man's face. "I used to treat him like a second son."

"Did you really think it was Biker?" Frank asked.

"I know Biker's a pretty wild young man, and the evidence at the trial was damaging. I almost believed he was guilty myself."

"What made you change your mind?" Joe asked.

"The calls kept coming even after Biker's escape. Knowing Biker, I expected him to head for Canada or Mexico. He wouldn't waste time calling up to threaten me."

"What exactly did the caller say?" Frank said.

Mr. Dalton rubbed his forehead as if trying to forget a bad dream. "The caller said he would return the watches for two hundred fifty thousand dollars, about half their value. If I didn't go through with the deal, he would kill Brandon and then me. I'm no coward, but this guy really scared me."

"Mr. Dalton hates guns. That's why he takes Trooper with him wherever he goes now," Sue added.

"When I heard voices, *male* voices, coming from Sue's office, I naturally thought the caller was about to make good on his threats," Mr. Dalton said. "I'm really sorry if Trooper frightened you, Joe."

"Forget it. No harm, no foul," Joe said lightly.

"Is Brandon okay?" Mr. Dalton asked Sue.

"He was before we left Bayport," Sue replied. "Why do you ask?"

"I can't get ahold of him. The hospital said he checked himself out, and there's no answer at the motel."

"Maybe he's at the police station giving a statement about Biker beating him up," Callie suggested.

"I can't believe that Biker attacked Brandon," Mr. Dalton said. "He knew Brandon wouldn't have a chance against him. This is very puzzling."

"Maybe what I've found could clear up some of the mystery," Frank said.

"I've always liked Biker," Mr. Dalton said. "I wish my own son had half his common sense. What have you found?"

"This should reopen the case and reverse Biker's conviction," Frank said. "Look here."

Joe, Callie, Sue, and Mr. Dalton gathered around Frank and the computer terminal.

"Here's Biker's original invoice sheet for the shipment of watches to Boston," Frank said. "Notice the date—March third, the day Biker left on his cross-country trip."

He handed the paper to Mr. Dalton, who looked the sheet over and nodded his head. Frank turned to his computer.

"But look at this." Frank played the computer

keys like a classical pianist. Seconds later a similar invoice sheet appeared on the screen.

Frank pointed to the screen. "Notice that the sales rep's code and invoice number are exactly the same as the numbers on Biker's invoice. But look here." Frank ran his finger straight across the screen to the date column.

"March thirtieth," Joe said.

"Right. Biker's original order wasn't shipped on March third—it went out the thirtieth."

"That's the day Biker returned from his trip," Joe said excitedly.

"And the day of the hijacking," Frank added.

"This date could be a typing error," Callie said.

"Maybe," Frank agreed, "except for *this*." He hit the keyboard again. Another form appeared on the screen.

"Biker's original invoice form!" Joe exclaimed.

"Right again. It was canceled on March fourth, the day *after* Biker left for his vacation." Frank punched the keys, and the two forms appeared side by side.

"Except for the date, they look exactly alike," Sue said.

"*Too* much alike," Frank said, "as if someone was trying to hide something." He turned to Mr. Dalton. "Do you often reroute shipments?"

"No. That's not the way I run my company,"

Scott Dalton said. "We process orders as they come in—unless I personally say otherwise. I don't like sales representatives stealing shipments from one another and routing them to special customers. It causes too much friction."

"Well, it looks as if that's what happened here. Biker's original shipment was headed to Boston," Joe said, pointing to the screen. "Then that same order got bumped back and routed to Kansas City!"

"Along the route of the hijacking!" Frank tapped on the desk.

"Then Biker is innocent," Joe said.

"How does this prove Biker's innocent?" Callie asked.

"Somebody changed Biker's order—setting it to go out on the thirtieth instead of the third," Frank explained. "That same person rerouted the shipment west instead of north. And all that time, *Biker was out of state*. He couldn't have known when the shipment left the plant or where it was going."

"Only two people could have known," Joe added. "The sales rep who rerouted the shipment and the driver of the truck, Nick Frost."

"I'd guess Frost set up the phony hijacking with the help of his Sinbad buddies," Frank concluded.

"Why?" asked Mr. Dalton.

"Frost was a heavy gambler and lost often,"

Joe explained. "Maybe he used up all his credit with Fat Harold and then started a new account, using Biker's name. When it came time to pay up, Frost dreamed up this hijacking scheme."

"But it didn't work out as planned," Frank added. "Somebody killed Frost."

"What?" Mr. Dalton said, shock in his voice.

"Before leaving Bayport, we were shot at and almost killed in a gas station fire," Joe said. "The police found Frost's body in a ditch nearby. They're holding Biker for the murder."

"I don't believe this," Mr. Dalton said as he sat down.

"Your theory sounds good," Callie said, "except for two things."

"What?" Joe asked, rounding on her.

"Who killed Frost, and who told Fat Harold we'd be at Frost's apartment?"

"According to Fat Harold," Frank said, "a little birdie told him. Maybe that same little birdie killed Frost."

"Isn't it funny how Sims always manages to be around whenever there's trouble?" Joe said thoughtfully.

Then his eyes widened. "Frank, we've got to get back to Bayport. If Sims is involved in any of this, Biker is in real trouble."

"Let me run a hard copy of these invoices to show to the police," Frank said as he began typing in commands on the computer.

Mr. Dalton stood, strength seeming to enter him. "I'll try to call Brandon and tell him to fire Sims, that you two have proof that Biker is innocent. Sims won't like it, though."

"He's got a real mean streak in him," Callie said.

"Mean?" Mr. Dalton said with a bitter laugh. "Sims's dead-or-alive reputation is no joke. Brandon told me that thirty percent of his fugitives are brought back in boxes. I'm sorry I was ever talked into hiring such a man."

"Callie, you'd better stay with Sue," Frank said as he pulled the black van into the motel parking lot. "If Sims is in on this, he might go after her, too."

"Sure," Callie replied. She and Sue hopped out of the van and headed for Sue's room.

Frank put the van in drive and started out of the parking lot.

"Hey, guys!" Brandon shouted as he pulled his cycle up next to the van. The swelling had gone down, but the bruises on his face were dark blue.

"Did your father get ahold of you?" Frank asked.

"Yeah. Sims is off the case. You guys did a great job."

"Where is Sims now?" Joe asked.

111

"He said something about leaving Bayport," Brandon replied.

"Keep an eye open for him," Frank warned. "We think he might be mixed up in all of this."

"Sure thing," Brandon said. "Say, where's this evidence you say you found?"

"Right here," Frank said, patting his shirt pocket.

"Great." Brandon gave him a smile.

"Tell Callie we're going home first, then to the police station," Frank said.

"You got it," Brandon said with a wave.

Frank pulled the van out of the parking lot and headed for home.

"If you hadn't broken the mobile phone, we could have warned Dad by now," Frank said with a smile.

"If you'll remember, it was your *girlfriend* who knocked me against that thing," Joe replied without humor.

Minutes later Frank and Joe were walking into their living room. Scuffling sounds came from the cellar.

"Dad's office!" Frank whispered.

They bolted down the stairs to Fenton Hardy's basement office. Biker, one handcuff around his wrist, was struggling with Sims for the bounty hunter's pistol.

"Sims!" Frank shouted.

Joe leapt at Biker.

The office echoed with the roar of the 9 mm automatic.

Sims jerked backward and crashed to the floor—lifeless.

Chapter

14

Joe was momentarily deafened by the blast of the gun. He watched Sims hit the floor, then lowered his shoulder and smashed into Biker, ignoring the pain from his hurt arm. With lightning speed he grabbed the gun and twisted it from Biker's hand.

Something whipped past Joe and slammed into Biker's chest. Biker doubled over and crumpled to the floor.

Joe spun around. The "dead" Sims stood in a karate stance.

"You're alive," Joe gasped.

"It looks that way," Sims replied. "Not that your friend didn't try his best."

"You *looked* dead," Frank said.

"That was the idea." Sims nodded at Joe. "Thanks for your help," he said with a smirk. The bounty hunter knelt next to Biker and holstered his gun. He grabbed Biker's arms and cuffed his hands. Biker groaned in pain as the cuffs clicked tighter and tighter.

"Hey! Those are too tight." Joe was furious.

"You don't think I'm going to give him a second chance, do you?" Sims asked. He lifted the groggy Biker and sat him in Fenton's chair. Frank was amazed at how the short, overweight Sims could move with such strength.

"What's Biker doing out of jail?" Joe asked, suddenly startled.

"Question your friend," Sims huffed.

"What happened, buddy?" Joe asked gently.

"I guess I got kind of stupid—I broke out," Biker answered, his speech thick.

"Why?" Frank was shocked. "Here we are trying to clear you and you make a break for it." He turned away and slapped his fist into the palm of his other hand.

"What can I say? I'm a dumb biker." Biker's head fell over on his chest again. He was out of it.

"Well, buddy, sorry, but as soon as you're better, we're going to have to return you to Con and the boys at the station."

"Over my dead body," Sims said.

"What do you mean? He has to go back," Frank stated simply.

"Look, kid, I found him after he escaped, and I'm taking him back to New York to collect my reward." An evil, triumphant smile cut into Sims's round, wrinkled face.

"You can't do that. He's being held on a murder charge here."

"What was that? I seem to have gone temporarily deaf. I couldn't hear a single word you said," Sims said, cupping a hand to his ear.

"I suppose you didn't get a phone call from Brandon, either?" Joe said.

"What call?" Sims asked.

"The one telling you to back off," Joe replied. "Why not check in with your boss?"

"Don't tell me what to do," Sims growled.

"Frank has found evidence that proves Biker didn't hijack that shipment of watches."

"Really?" Sims said with a mocking look.

Frank took the two invoices from his pocket and handed them to Sims. He quickly explained Biker's vacation schedule and the rerouting of the watches.

"It was impossible for Biker to know where and when those watches would go out," Joe concluded.

Sims looked at both invoices. He rubbed the back of his neck and then asked, "Get these from a computer, Frank?"

"From Sue's computer at the watch company," Frank replied.

"You're pretty good with a computer, aren't you, Frank? I bet you'd do just about anything for a friend, wouldn't you?" Sims's steel gray eyes bored into Frank.

Joe glanced at Frank, then at Sims. He knew what Sims was implying.

"Frank didn't tamper with those invoices," Joe said, controlling his slowly rising anger.

Sims threw up his hands in mock protest and handed the invoices back to Frank. "What can I say?"

"There's something else you should know," Frank said. "Biker didn't beat up Brandon."

"Just how do you know that?" Sims asked, curious in spite of himself.

Frank walked over to Biker, who was still unconscious. He gently lifted Biker's hands and turned them over.

"See here?" he said. "No bruises."

"Huh?" Sims looked confused.

"You saw Brandon at the hospital," Frank said. "Whoever gave him that beating would have some badly bruised knuckles."

"Unless the attacker was wearing motorcycle gloves," Sims countered.

"I've seen the difference between someone beaten with gloves and someone beaten with bare knuckles," Frank said confidently. "Brandon was beaten with bare fists, and he was beaten by Frost.''

"Impossible!" Sims shook his head in disbelief.

"Remember how badly scraped Frost's knuckles were?" Frank asked.

"That's right!" Joe said.

"What would Brandon have to do with Frost?" Sims asked.

"I don't know, but I want to ask Brandon about Frost, and I want to find out why he lied to us about calling you," Frank replied.

"You two will have to follow that up by yourselves," Sims said. "As soon as Conway revives, I'm taking him back to Queens."

"What kind of detective are you?" Joe was incredulous.

"I'm the best detective there is, sonny boy." Sims's eyes flashed with anger and his cheeks turned a dark red. "I do my job. I was hired to bring Conway in. And I don't know anything about a murder charge here. Got that?" Sims grabbed his rumpled hat. "I just stopped in to say goodbye to Fenton and pay him for his services."

"Where *is* Dad?" Frank asked, hoping to slow Sims down.

"Don't know. 'Bye." Sims grabbed Biker's arm and tried to pull him from the chair. Biker groaned. Joe pushed Sims aside. Both squared off.

"Move off, buddy boy," Sims growled at Joe.

Frank was about to help Joe when the phone rang. He grabbed the receiver, keeping an eye on the other two.

"Hello," he said.

"Frank!" It was Callie, her voice high and shaky.

Frank was about to ask Callie what was wrong when he heard scuffling noises in the background—and then the unmistakable voice of Fat Harold.

"Is this Frank Hardy of Acme Speedy Delivery?" Fat Harold wheezed into the phone.

"What do you want?"

From the dark scowl on Frank's face, Joe knew something was wrong. He forgot about Sims and stood next to his older brother. Frank punched the speaker phone so Joe could hear.

"I've got two special delivery packages for you. They're extremely fragile. One is Callie Shaw, the other is Sue Murphy."

"Let them go," Frank ordered.

"Oh, I'll let them go," Fat Harold replied. "But *how* I let them go depends on you."

"What do you mean by that?" Frank asked.

"We're at a junkyard just outside of Bayport. And Rock—you remember Rock, don't you, Frank?—he's always wanted to play with one of those car crushers. Right now he's got Miss Shaw and Miss Murphy in the front seat of a rusty old

119

Ford. He's just dying to push the button that will turn the car into one cubic foot of metal."

"No!" Frank yelled.

"I knew you'd want these special packages." Fat Harold paused and breathed in deeply. "I want one of three things—the two hundred and fifty grand that Biker Conway owes me, the watches he stole, or Conway himself."

"Where? When?"

"Bruce's Paradise Salvage. Know where it is?"

"Yes."

"Thirty minutes, or Rock pushes the button. It's a fair trade, Frank. You get two, while I only get one."

"We can't get any of those things together that fast," Frank protested.

"Twenty-nine minutes and forty-three seconds," Fat Harold said. "Or your girlfriend becomes just another small part of American culture."

Fat Harold's screeching laugh tore at Frank's ears until he slammed down the receiver.

Frank dashed from the room, but reentered instantly. "Sims, you wait here with Biker, or you're dead. You got that—dead!"

Chapter

15

BRUCE'S PARADISE SALVAGE looked like anything but a paradise. A crazy maze of rust-eaten cars, engine parts, and transmissions littered the pot-holed dirt road. The dead smell of wet and rotting upholstery filled the air.

"One minute," Frank said.

Joe nodded.

They jogged toward the rear of the salvage yard. Joe carried a largish black briefcase under his right arm, and he tried not to let his injured left arm swing out too much.

Darkness had set in, and the salvage yard's single streetlight cast deep shadows. Frank and Joe kept their eyes on the shadows, wary that Fat Harold could have set a trap for them.

They turned a corner of stacked cars to find Callie and Sue flanked by Rock and Hard Place, who held two ugly automatics leveled at the girls.

"Freeze," ordered Rock. He shoved his gun into Callie's side.

Callie grimaced.

"Be careful with that thing." Frank's voice was tight. "We brought what you wanted." He looked around. "Where's your boss?"

"I'm here, remembering the good old days," Fat Harold called to Frank and Joe. He stepped out from behind a faded yellow school bus.

"I didn't think they had buses in reform school," Joe said.

Fat Harold laughed. He nodded to his two thugs. Rock and Hard Place locked and loaded their automatics. They pointed the deadly pieces at the heads of Callie and Sue.

"Wait!" Frank yelled.

Fat Harold walked till he stood about ten yards from Frank. He looked at his watch.

"Right on time. Excellent." He glanced at the briefcase under Joe's arm. "I assume you have either the money, the watches, or Conway in that little case." His nasal laugh bounced off the rusted cars.

"Money," Joe replied without a smile. "Two hundred and fifty thousand."

"Very good," Fat Harold wheezed.

"Biker has confessed to stealing the watches,

then fencing them and hiding the money until he could get out of the country. It's all here." Joe tossed the case at Fat Harold's feet.

Fat Harold jumped back.

"There's no booby trap," Frank assured the bookie.

"How did you know where to find Callie and Sue?" Joe asked at almost the same time.

"I've got friends I never knew I had," Fat Harold began as he kicked at the briefcase. "The same little birdie that warned me to go to Frost's apartment told me Conway's girlfriend was staying at the Bayport Motel." He nodded back to Callie. "And she's the insurance I needed to make sure you two wouldn't try anything funny."

Fat Harold knelt down. He lifted the briefcase and smiled as he pushed down on the snaps. His face reddened.

"It's locked," he growled.

"Oh, sorry," Frank replied. "I've got the key." He put his hand into his jeans pocket. Rock turned his automatic on Frank, who quickly raised both hands to show he had no weapon.

"Slowly," Fat Harold said.

Frank pulled a small silver key from his pocket and held it up.

"Throw me the key or say goodbye to one of the girls." Fat Harold's face tightened with rage.

"One girl, one key," Frank said calmly, gambling that Fat Harold wouldn't order his two thugs to shoot Callie and Sue.

Fat Harold's face untwisted into a thin smile.

"Fair enough," the bookie replied. He nodded to Hard Place. The thug lowered his automatic and pushed Sue toward Frank.

Fat Harold laughed. "The little birdie told me that Callie Shaw means a lot to Frank Hardy. We'll hold her until we're safely out of Bayport. Now the key, if you please."

"Don't do it, Frank," Joe said. "Make them give up Callie."

"Kid, don't make a fatal mistake," Fat Harold said. "Don't get the foolish idea you can *make* me do anything. He held out his hand. "The key—*now!*"

Frank flipped the key at Fat Harold. The bookie picked it up and put it in one of the locks. He gently turned it. Frank heard a small sigh escape from the bookie when nothing happened. Fat Harold put the key in the second lock and turned it. He smiled triumphantly and lifted the briefcase lid.

Frank shoved Sue to the ground as he and Joe covered their eyes. A blinding light burst from the briefcase. Fat Harold screamed as the scorching glare of a caseful of exploding flashbulbs tore into his eyes.

Frank and Joe charged. Frank leapt for Rock. He was relieved to see that Callie, even though blinded, had thrown herself to the ground and was scrambling away from the thug. Rock was shaking his head and swinging his arms wildly in front of him. Frank landed a solid kick to Rock's stomach. The thug sat down—hard. Even so, he raised his gun, aiming blindly in the direction of his attacker. Frank kicked the gun from Rock's hand and rammed a fist into the side of the thug's head. Rock hit the ground and didn't move.

At the same moment Joe ran for Fat Harold, who was staggering and screaming, one hand over his eyes, the other trying to pull a pistol from his pocket. Joe whipped a sawed-off baseball bat from his sling and tapped Fat Harold's wrist as he came up with the gun. The gun went flying, and Joe sent the bookie flying in the opposite direction. Then he turned to Hard Place.

The thug, tears streaming from his blinded eyes, began firing his automatic wildly in the direction of any sound. Frank and Joe hit the ground.

"Stay down!" Frank yelled to Callie and Sue.

Hard Place turned toward the sound of Frank's voice and squeezed off a shot. Frank rolled away from the slug as it sliced the ground inches away from him.

A single pistol shot pierced the air. Hard Place was knocked to the ground as a bullet slammed into his shoulder.

Sims and a handcuffed Biker ran from behind a

stack of cars. Sims's 9 mm was still smoking from the shot he'd fired at the thug.

Just then Rock staggered to his feet, a backup gun in his hand. He had apparently regained his eyesight and was aiming the pistol at Mort Sims.

"Sims!" Frank yelled. He was too far away to help the bounty hunter.

Suddenly Biker knocked a surprised Sims to one side and sprinted toward Rock. He lowered his shoulder and slammed into the thug with such force that Rock was lifted from the ground and flew several feet backward before smashing into a stack of rusted cars. The unconscious gunman slid to the ground in a lump, his pistol landing harmlessly a few feet away.

"You all right?" Biker asked as he helped Sims up.

"Yeah," Sims replied. He shoved Biker's hands away and stood on his own.

"You could say thanks," Joe said as he helped Sue to her feet.

"Conway's lucky I didn't shoot him," Sims said. "I thought he was trying to escape."

"Good job," Frank said to Callie, who had wiped her eyes and was now brushing dirt from her jeans.

Sirens cut through the air. Moments later several Bayport police cars pulled into the salvage yard. Con Riley and Fenton Hardy hopped from the lead car.

"Frank! Joe! Are you okay?" Fenton asked as he ran up to his sons.

"Sure, Dad," Frank replied. He turned to Con. "Better have your men cuff these three."

Riley nodded to the other officers.

"We've got proof that Biker didn't know about the watch shipment," Joe said as he handed the invoices to Fenton. He explained about the trip to Queens and finding the invoice with the re-routed watches.

"That adds up with what Con found," Fenton replied.

"What's that?"

"The wallet and driver's license found at the scene of Frost's murder were reported stolen several months ago by Biker," Fenton said.

"That's right," Biker added as he joined the group. "I lost my wallet during a Riding on Time tour."

"He could have pretended to lose it," Sims insisted.

"Maybe," Fenton said. "But Frost was murdered by someone riding a cycle. When Biker was arrested, he was on foot."

"He could have ditched the bike anywhere," Sims retorted. "And what about his debts?" He turned to face Joe. "You told me yourself that Fat Harold was after Conway for not paying up on his gambling debts."

"I never gamble," Biker replied. "That's a fool's game."

"Never? We'll see about that." Sims stalked over to a patrol car and pulled Fat Harold from the back. He marched the bookie toward the group and stood him in front of Biker.

Fat Harold, still dazed, looked Biker up and down.

"What am I doing? Judging a beauty contest?" the bookie sneered.

"This is the man who owes you two hundred and fifty grand," Sims insisted. "This is Biker Conway."

"No," Fat Harold replied.

"That flash-bomb must have blinded you," Sims said in disbelief.

"Excuse me," Fat Harold said indignantly. "I know the faces of everyone who owes me money, especially big money." He pointed at Biker. "And this guy is *not* the Biker Conway I know!"

Chapter

16

"I WAS WRONG," Brandon Dalton said as he stood in the Hardys' living room, trying to avoid Biker's eyes. "Frank's right. Frost did beat me up, but he said Biker had paid him to do it."

"You knew I couldn't stand Frost," Biker said.

"I wasn't thinking."

"Why did you lie to us about calling Sims off the case?" Joe asked.

"I didn't say I had gotten ahold of Sims," Brandon replied. "What I meant at the motel was that I agreed with my dad about kicking him off the case."

"None of this makes any sense," Sims said.

"Why?" Joe asked. "Because you might have the wrong man?"

129

Sims glared at Joe. Joe smiled.

"Did you disguise yourself when you placed your bets with Fat Harold?" Sims asked Biker with a cold stare.

"Get off his case," Joe hissed.

"That's all right, Joe," Biker said with a smile. He returned Sims's stare. "It doesn't matter whether you believe me or not. I'm innocent. I know it—more important, my friends know it. And tomorrow the courts will know it."

"And I'll drop my assault charges," Brandon added.

"You can take off those handcuffs," Joe said to Sims.

"You've got to be kidding," Sims chuckled. "I've got my reward money to collect."

"Biker's innocent and you know it," Joe insisted. Joe didn't get anywhere with Sims so he turned to Fenton. "I give my word. Biker won't go anywhere."

Fenton looked at his son. "Uncuff him," he said to Sims.

"Not on your life."

"For a professional, you've acted pretty foolishly," Fenton said without hesitation. "Frank and Joe have proved that Biker didn't hijack the truck, the murder charges have been dropped, and Brandon has just admitted that it was Frost who beat him up." Fenton walked up to Sims. "You're in my home, and I'm not going to let you keep cuffs on an innocent man. Tomorrow we'll go to court, and I know with a good word from us any judge will drop the charges against Biker for escaping. I think you're out of your money, anyway, Mort."

Fuming, Sims stomped over to Biker and unlocked the cuffs.

"Thanks," Biker said sincerely as he rubbed his chafed wrists.

Sims turned to Fenton. "There's still something about this case that isn't right."

"Well, it's time you used your detecting skills to help and not hinder this investigation," Fenton said.

Sims rubbed his neck. He was visibly embarrassed.

"I suggest we question Fat Harold," Fenton added.

Sims lowered his head and walked out the front door.

"You sure Callie and Sue will be okay at the motel?" Fenton asked before leaving.

"Con Riley said he'd post a patrol car outside," Frank replied.

"Besides, I'll be there," Brandon added as he put on his motorcycle helmet.

"Biker, I'm glad my sons were able to prove you innocent," Fenton said as he shook Biker's hand. "I'll call if we get anything out of Fat Harold."

"I'm lucky to have you two on my side," Biker said after Fenton and Brandon left.

"Three now," Joe said. "Didn't you hear my dad call you 'Biker'? He's never done that before."

"Yeah," Biker replied. "I could be in jail on a murder charge. Any lawyer could have convinced a jury that I knew Frost had framed me and that I killed him in a blind rage. He must have lifted my wallet months ago."

"Who could hate you enough to frame you for the hijacking and the murder?" Frank asked.

Biker shrugged his shoulders. "Beats me. What I want to know is who pretended to be me when he placed all those bets with Fat Harold."

"Does Sue have an ex-boyfriend who could be jealous?" Joe asked.

"Not that I know of," Biker replied.

"We can ask Sue about that tomorrow morning. Right now, I say we get some rest," Frank said as he headed for bed. "No telling how long my dad and Sims will be with Fat Harold."

"You can sleep in Aunt Gertrude's room," Joe said to Biker. "I hope you like perfume."

As they reached the top of the stairs, Biker turned to Joe and said, "I'll understand if you want to lock the doors and windows."

"What?" Joe asked, astonished. Then he saw the grin on Biker's face. He jabbed Biker in the shoulder. "You'd make a wisecrack to the devil."

Joe slept restlessly, disturbed by strange dreams. The worst one had him trying to prevent Biker from riding off a large cliff into a bottomless grave. The night seemed to go on forever.

He heard a noise in his bedroom and sat up. "Who's there?" he said loudly.

"It's me," Frank replied.

Joe jumped from his bed. "Did Dad call?"

"Keep your voice down. They got here about an hour ago and went to bed. Sims is staying, too."

"What time is it?"

"Almost five-thirty. Get dressed."

"Why are you whispering?" Joe asked as he pulled on his jeans.

"I think I'm onto something, and I don't want to wake Biker."

"What is it?"

"Shhh. In the basement." Frank left Joe's room.

Joe didn't like it when Frank started acting secretive. Joe preferred the straight approach. Frank liked to keep his ideas to himself until he was absolutely sure that he was right. Sometimes he waited until it was almost too late.

Frank had his computer booted up by the time Joe reached the basement office.

Like Joe, Frank had slept restlessly. But his restlessness was because of a nagging problem—Fat Harold's "little birdie." Someone had always been one step ahead of the Hardys and had nearly gotten them killed twice. Joe suspected Sims. But it would have been easier for Sims to kill Biker in the "line of duty." No, Fat Harold's "little birdie" had to be someone who was close to Biker and to Frank and Joe as well.

"What's the big mystery?" Joe asked. He sat in the chair next to Frank's and rubbed the sleep from his eyes.

"How did Fat Harold know someone would be at Frost's apartment—and where to find Callie and Sue?" Frank asked.

"Someone told him," Joe answered with a yawn.

"Right—his 'little birdie.' And how did that little birdie tell him?"

Joe sat up. "What do you mean?"

"How did the little birdie contact Fat Harold?"

"By phone!"

"Right, again. Someone's been keeping tabs on us and reporting back to Fat Harold. And now for the grand prize: What kind of phone calls did the little birdie make?"

"Long distance!"

"Give the man a stuffed bear!" Frank said. Just then the computer chirped and the screen lit up. "The little birdie made two calls to Fat Harold. If he was close enough to know our every move, then he had—"

"To make the calls from Bayport," Joe finished.

"You win the bonus prize," Frank said. He turned to his computer and began punching in the code numbers for accessing long-distance phone calls.

"Sims could have known," Joe said.

"No. Whoever made the first call tried to set us up. Sims didn't know we were going to Queens. The second phone call was to inform Fat Harold about Callie and Sue and set us up again. Fat Harold was in Bayport shortly after we arrived—and we were with Sims the whole time."

The computer beeped, and Frank punched the Enter button. "Aha?" he said triumphantly.

"What is it?" Joe moved to view the screen. A seemingly endless list of phone numbers rolled before his eyes.

Frank hit a button and the list stopped scrolling. He pointed at one line. "Here's the first phone call."

"How can you tell?"

"Remember Fat Harold's crazy number?"

"Yeah. Five-five-five-BETS," Joe replied.

"BETS translates to two-three-eight-seven—and there it is."

"Here's the second," Joe said, pointing farther down the screen.

"The time of the first call was shortly before noon, about the time we were on our way to Queens. The second call was made several hours later, just after we got back to Bayport."

"The two phone calls came from different phones," Joe said with disappointment. "Probably pay phones."

"Let's find out." Frank punched in the first and second phone numbers. A second later the screen flashed with the answers.

"One's an extension at Bayport Hospital; the other is a room at the Bayport Motel," Joe said.

Frank turned to Joe. "Are you thinking what I'm thinking?"

"If I am, then Sue and Callie are in danger," Joe replied.

"Let's be sure." Frank picked up the phone next to his computer and dialed the hospital number. The nurse on duty refused to give out any information about the extension number. Frank next dialed the Bayport Motel. The phone seemed to ring endlessly.

Finally a groggy voice answered, "Hello?"

It was Brandon Dalton.

"Sorry, wrong number," Frank said quickly and hung up the phone.

"Dalton," Joe said as fact.

"The *B* on the road map stood for Brandon, not Biker," Frank added.

"We'd better wake up Dad and Sims," Frank said.

The Hardys turned to leave, then froze. Biker stood in the doorway. Joe had never seen such rage on a human face. His friend appeared to be out of his mind with anger.

"Biker—" Joe began.

Before Joe could finish his sentence, Biker Conway slammed the door shut with such force that it cracked. Frank and Joe could hear him running up the stairs.

Joe was the first to reach the door. He pushed, but the door wouldn't budge.

"It's jammed," he yelled to Frank.

"Stand back," Frank shouted. Joe stood to one side as Frank ran and jumped at the door. His karate kick split the door in half, and he and Joe rushed up the stairs.

They were stunned to see the kitchen table and chairs scattered, as if someone had thrown them around the room. Under one upended chair lay Sims.

Frank picked up the chair. A quickly swelling bruise was taking shape below Sims's right eye.

"Biker," the bounty hunter yelled. "He's gone insane!"

A car engine roared to life outside. Joe ran to the doorway in time to see Biker peel away from the curb in Fenton's car.

"The motel," Frank shouted as he ran to the van.

Frank and Joe jumped aboard, Frank shoving the key into the ignition. But nothing happened.

"He's killed the engine," Frank yelled, slamming his fist against the dash.

Joe hopped out, ran to the front, and threw open the hood. "He ripped out some spark plug wires."

"Great," Frank said. "Are they on the ground?"

"No, he must have taken them with him." Joe slammed the hood closed. Then he yelled, "What about Sims's car?"

They dashed back to the kitchen, to find Fenton Hardy kneeling over Sims, who was still trying to pull himself together. When he heard the whole story, Fenton dug into Sims's pockets himself to find the car keys.

His face was gray as he passed the keys to his sons. "You'd better find Biker quickly," he said, pointing to the stunned bounty hunter's empty holster.

"Biker left the keys, but he took Sims's gun."

Chapter

17

THE BATTERED CHEVY screeched to a stop just outside Brandon's motel room. The door stood wide open. Fenton Hardy's car was parked in the space right in front.

The door to Sue's room flew open and Sue ran out, followed by Callie.

"Your father just phoned," Sue said, sobbing, as Frank and Joe hopped from the car.

Joe grabbed her by the shoulders. "Where's Biker?" he shouted.

"H-h-he showed up a few minutes ago. He told Brandon he wanted to show him where the pits were." Sue burst into tears.

Joe shook her. "Did you see a gun?"

Sue's eyes widened. "No."

"How did they leave?" Frank asked.

"They took Brandon's bike," Callie replied.

Joe threw his sling off. "Give me your keys," he said, flexing his arm. Sue pulled her bike keys from her pocket. Joe grabbed them and ran to Sue's cycle.

"Where do you think you're going?" Frank yelled after his brother. "Your arm—you can't drive a bike."

Joe kicked the cycle to life. "Watch me. Follow me in Sims's car. We're going to the pits." He shifted to first and zoomed out of the parking lot.

Frank, Callie, and Sue hopped in Sims's Chevy and followed. Joe quickly became a small dot to them and then disappeared altogether.

Joe was at the pits in a matter of minutes. He shot through the entrance and guided the cycle around potholes and gravel mounds. He knew that Biker's favorite practice spot was the largest hole near the rear of the quarry. It was also the most secluded. Nice place for a murder, Joe thought.

A gunshot echoed throughout the quarry. Joe gunned the throttle and jumped a ridge. Before the echo of the shot had died, he'd stopped the cycle at the edge of the large pit and shut the engine off. He gasped.

Biker was on his knees, a widening stain of red on his shirt. Brandon stood over Biker waving two weapons—Sims's 9 mm and a snubnose .38

pistol. Joe recognized the .38 as the same gun that had been fired at them at the gas station. Brandon was shouting hysterically at the slumping Biker.

"Then my old man cut my salary after you finked on me about the salesmen phoning in. He said he was going to fire me if I fouled up again. I'm the son of the company's owner. I have an image to maintain. Frost promised me some easy money—fast. And, yeah, I used your name. You're just a low-life mechanic who tried to be a big shot."

Brandon paced back and forth in front of Biker, swinging his arms wildly. Biker fell to his side. Brandon grabbed Biker's collar and pulled him up.

"It was easy to talk Frost into pulling the hijacking while you were away. But why should I pay Fat Harold? He thought Biker Conway owed him the money. By planting your wallet next to Frost's body, I made sure that you'd be blamed for the murder, too."

Brandon laughed and let Biker fall to the ground.

"I'm the only one who knows where the watches are. My dad's company will get the insurance money, but I'll be able to live up to my image after I sell the watches."

He aimed the two pistols at Biker.

"Of course, you'll have to die. I'll plead self-defense. After all, everyone from Bayport to Queens knows about your hot temper.''

Brandon locked the hammers of the guns. An evil grin crossed his face.

Joe kicked the bike to life, jerked the throttle open, and flew down the hill. Brandon turned, his face twisted in confusion and fear. He fired wildly at Joe. Joe zigzagged the bike so Brandon couldn't draw a bead on him.

Brandon seemed to realize he was wasting bullets. He threw the .38 aside, crouched in a shooting position, and carefully aimed the 9 mm at the onrushing Joe.

Joe ducked low over the cycle and let up on the throttle. He stomped on the rear brake and turned the bike to the left, skidding into Brandon. The rich kid jerked backward as the 9 mm roared. His bullet whizzed past Joe's head, knocking Joe from his bike and slamming him into the hard ground on his left arm. Pain from his earlier injury shot through his body like a thousand volts of electricity.

Brandon took the opportunity to run. As Joe lay dazed, Dalton hopped on his bike and sped away.

Joe stood and stumbled toward the bleeding Biker. Biker, his eyes glazed, pointed after Brandon.

"Get him," he gasped, then fainted.

Joe jerked his bike up and kicked it into a roar.

He twisted the throttle and rocketed after the fleeing Brandon. Brandon wasn't a good rider—slowly but steadily, Joe closed the gap.

Desperately, Brandon fired the gun at Joe. The recoil nearly made him lose control of his cycle. When the gun emptied, he threw it at Joe, missing widely. He jumped a small hill and almost flipped the cycle.

Joe expertly jumped the hill, moving ever closer to Brandon.

The hills in this part of the quarry were more numerous and higher. With each jump, Joe narrowed the gap. On the steepest grade, Joe was able to pull up on Brandon's right side.

Brandon kicked out. Joe swerved aside, but quickly caught up to Brandon again.

Joe pulled his cycle slightly ahead of Brandon's. He reached over, grabbed the front brake handle, and squeezed. The bike jolted to a stop and flipped Brandon forward. He screamed as he flew through the air and slammed into a mound of gravel. His cycle flipped end over end, flying dangerously close to Joe. Joe swerved his cycle to the right. Brandon's bike crashed into a boulder and died with a screaming whine.

Joe turned his cycle and headed toward Brandon, who was shaken but not seriously hurt.

"On your feet," Joe ordered.

Brandon stood slowly on wobbly legs. He shook his head and stumbled.

"Let's go," Joe growled.

Brandon staggered forward with Joe following on the cycle.

Moments later, they returned to their starting place. Joe was glad to see Frank and Callie giving first aid to Biker.

"How's he doing?" Joe asked, concern in his voice.

"He'll survive," Frank replied. "Sue's gone to call an ambulance." He looked up at Brandon. "I see you got him."

"Not without a fight," Joe said. He hopped from the cycle and knelt next to Biker.

"Hey, hotshot!" Biker tried to laugh, but ended up groaning.

"Take it easy," Joe said.

"Great." Biker grimaced.

Callie picked up the .38 by the trigger guard. "Whose is this?"

"That's Brandon's." Joe took the gun from Callie. "Recognize it, Frank?"

"Sure. Well, I should; it looks like the gun from the gas station."

Joe wrapped the gun in a handkerchief. "I also heard what Brandon said to you, Biker, and I'll repeat it at his trial."

"Good work, Joe." Frank shook his head. "But I wish you'd waited for the rest of us."

"If I'd waited for you to catch up," Joe protested, "Biker might be dead."

"He still might be!" called out a tinny voice from the top of the hill.

They turned to see Fat Harold aiming a MAC-10 submachine gun at the group.

His nasal laugh echoed through the pits as he squeezed the trigger, sending a blizzard of bullets at Frank, Joe, Callie, Sue, and Biker.

Chapter

18

"I KNEW THAT would get your attention." Fat Harold giggled as he trotted down the hill. He'd purposely aimed high over their heads. The bookie stopped just short of the group, covering them with his MAC-10. "Why the surprised look, friends? You may be on the side of law and order, but I own the keys to the courthouse. It's good business to have a few state judges on your payroll. One of them owed me, and I'm out. Although I couldn't get my friends out."

Fat Harold laughed and moved toward the frightened Brandon.

"So, I catch up with you at last, *Biker Conway*." Fat Harold leveled the gun at Brandon's heart as the kid cowered. "Or should I say *Brandon Dalton?*"

"N-n-no," Brandon whimpered.

"Sorry," Fat Harold said. "But you don't have the watches or the money. So I'll have to write off the debt—and erase you as well." He nodded to the others. "And I'm sorry that you five will have to join young Mr. Dalton in the bad debt column. I can't have any witnesses. You do understand."

Fat Harold gave them his thin-lipped smile as he worked the bolt on his gun. Brandon stepped back, his hands in front of him as though they could stop the lead slugs. His face was a portrait of terror.

"All bets are off." Fat Harold laughed. "It's time to cash in your chips." He stepped forward, his finger tightening on the trigger.

That step forward brought the bookie to the spot where Biker lay. In a desperate move, Biker lashed out in a kick. Fat Harold screamed as his knees buckled. As the bookie was thrown off balance, his MAC-10 sprayed shells wildly into the dirt. Brandon fell to the ground.

The Hardys moved quickly, Joe yanking the gun from Fat Harold's hands while Frank landed a powerful uppercut to the bookie's jaw. Fat Harold groaned and slithered to the ground, unconscious.

Callie ran to Brandon and turned him over.

"He's okay," she yelled back to Frank and Joe. "I think he just fainted."

"Good," Frank replied.

"Not so good," Joe said as he knelt beside Biker. "He's reopened his wound—and he's in danger of bleeding to death."

"And because of Joe's statement, Brandon's been booked for the murder of Frost and for hijacking the watches," Fenton Hardy said as Sue was adjusting the pillow behind Biker's head.

Biker shifted on the hospital bed. "Too bad," he said. He was startled by the stunned looks Frank and Joe gave him. "For all his faults, I kind of liked the kid. He was good for a few laughs around the office."

"How long are you going to be in here?" Mort Sims asked. He leaned against the door, crumpled hat in hand.

"Doc says about a week," Biker replied.

"Well," Mort Sims said as he put on his hat, "this is one time I'm glad I didn't bring back my man." He opened the door. "See you around, Fenton." Then he was gone.

"That guy has some nerve," Frank said.

"It's the closest you'll get to an apology," Fenton said. He faced Frank and Joe. "And you two—"

"Dad, I'm sorry if I caused you any trouble," Frank said.

"Yeah, I know I said some things that—" Joe began.

"Forget it," Fenton interrupted. "If I had to lose a case, I'm glad I lost it to my sons." He headed for the door. "I'm off to the airport to pick up your mother and Aunt Gertrude. You two be home in time for supper."

"As long as it's anything but frozen fish sticks," Joe said with a grin.

Fenton shook his head and left the room.

"You're going back to Queens after you get out?" Frank asked Biker.

"Right." Biker grinned. "The D.A. is making a motion tomorrow to drop all charges. Then I'll be returning to DalTime."

"Why?" asked Callie. "Dalton caused all your problems."

"*Brandon* Dalton caused all my problems," Biker replied. "Brandon even talked his dad into hiring Sims."

"Why?" asked Callie.

"Because Brandon figured Biker wouldn't make it back to Queens," Joe said.

"Brandon even had himself beaten up," Frank added. "And then he killed Frost to shut his mouth about the watches and the beating."

"But why are you going back to DalTime?" Callie asked.

Biker looked at Sue. "I like Mr. Dalton. He's

going to need all the support Sue and I can give him."

"Besides," Sue added, "we need our jobs if we're going to get married. Speaking of which, we'll have to set a new date. But you guys are definitely invited to the wedding."

"You've got it," Joe said with a grin. "Just do me a favor."

"Name it." Biker grinned back at him.

"When we turn up for the wedding—no adventures. Okay?"

Biker nodded solemnly. "You have my word. My wedding will be as quiet as my homecoming."

Callie, Frank, and Sue cracked up. But Joe just shook his head gloomily.

"That's what I'm afraid of," he said.

Frank and Joe's next case:

The Hardys fly to Halifax, Canada, to check out an insurance scam. But as they leave the airport their car is sprayed with bullets. Soon the brother detectives discover they're number one on somebody's hit list.

First a friend of their father's is seriously hurt in a bomb blast. Then one of their suspects winds up dead. What started out as a white-collar crime has become an all-out war. And unless the young sleuths track down the stunning secret behind the vicious attacks—they'll be crossing the border in a body bag . . . in *Countdown to Terror,* Case #28 in The Hardy Boys Casefiles™.

Forthcoming Titles in the
Hardy Boys™ Casefiles Series

Books in The Nancy Drew™ Series

Simon & Schuster publish a wide range of titles from pre-school books to books for adults.

For up-to-date catalogues, please contact:

International Book Distributors
Campus 400
Maylands Avenue
Hemel Hempstead
Herts
HP2 7EZ

Tel. 0442 882255